OUTNUMBERED. . . .

Carver laughed, an icy, brittle burst laced with contempt. "You're one man against thirty. My boys will cut you down where you stand."

"I'd get off a shot or two," Fargo said. "At you."

Carver's free hand was clenching and unclenching as if he yearned to clamp it around Fargo's throat. "The last time someone had the nerve to buck me, I had him tied to a tree and whipped. Don't make the same mistake. If I want to manhandle my servant, I will. If I want to wipe out the Pawnee, I will. No one defies me. Ever."

Fargo's right hand flashed so swiftly that the Colt was out and cocked and the muzzle pressed against Carver's forehead before anyone else could so much as blink. "For the last time. Let go of him or buck out in gore. . . ."

THE
TRAILSMAN
#226

NEBRASKA
SLAYING
GROUND

by

Jon Sharpe

A SIGNET BOOK

SIGNET
Published by New American Library, a division of
Penguin Putnam Inc., 375 Hudson Street,
New York, New York 10014, U.S.A.
Penguin Books Ltd, 27 Wrights Lane,
London W8 5TZ, England
Penguin Books Australia Ltd, Ringwood,
Victoria, Australia
Penguin Books Canada Ltd, 10 Alcorn Avenue,
Toronto, Ontario, Canada M4V 3B2
Penguin Books (N.Z.) Ltd, 182–190 Wairau Road,
Auckland 10, New Zealand

Penguin Books Ltd, Registered Offices:
Harmondsworth, Middlesex, England

First published by Signet, an imprint of New American Library,
a division of Penguin Putnam Inc.

First Printing, August 2000
10 9 8 7 6 5 4 3 2 1

The first chapter of this book previously appeared in *Prairie Firestorm*,
the two hundred twenty-fifth volume in this series.

 REGISTERED TRADEMARK—MARCA REGISTRADA

Printed in the United States of America

PUBLISHER'S NOTE
This is a work of fiction. Names, characters, places, and incidents either
are the product of the author's imagination or are used fictitiously,
and any resemblance to actual persons, living or dead, business establishments, events, or locales is entirely coincidental.

The Trailsman

Beginnings ... they bend the tree and they mark the man. Skye Fargo was born when he was eighteen. Terror was his midwife, vengeance his first cry. Killing spawned Skye Fargo, ruthless, cold-blooded murder. Out of the acrid smoke of gunpowder still hanging in the air, he rose, cried out a promise never forgotten.

The Trailsman they began to call him all across the West: searcher, scout, hunter, the man who could see where others only looked, his skills for hire but not his soul, the man who lived each day to the fullest, yet trailed each tomorrow. Skye Fargo, the Trailsman, the seeker who could take the wildness of a land and the wanting of a woman and make them his own.

1861—along the winding course of the Platte River, where money could spirit one's fortunes to fame and wealth—or lead one down the quick road to harsh death. . . .

1

"You can touch me if you like."

Skye Fargo stopped in front of the lovely dove who had invited him to sample her wares, his lake blue eyes dancing with mirth. He openly admired her hourglass figure, sheathed in a tight red dress that accented her abundant charms. "Just like that?" he asked. A big, broad-shouldered man in buckskins, he dwarfed the woman's petite frame.

"It's customary," the dove said, nodding to the right and the left. "See for yourself."

The long entrance hall to Bob Potee's gambling den on the second floor of number 3 Missouri Avenue was lined by buxom beauties. As patrons walked by, they touched the lovely lady of their choice where no man had any business touching a lady except in private. But the women didn't seem to mind. In fact, they were enjoying themselves immensely. Joking and laughing, they thrust their bosoms out in flagrant invitation.

"It's done for luck at the gaming tables," the dove explained. "Mr. Potee started the custom when he opened the place." Her voice lowered and she winked slyly. "Of course, you'll have even better luck if you slip me a twenty-dollar gold piece."

Fargo laughed. "Sorry, gorgeous. I'd love to oblige, but I barely have twenty dollars to my name." He'd lost most of his poke the night before in a stud poker game at another one of Kansas City's landmarks, Doc Frame's Gambling Emporium. The city boasted upward of twenty such establishments and was well on its way to becoming the gambling capital of the entire West.

The dove took the news in stride. "Tell you what," she said, studying him from head to toe. "It's on the house. Treat yourself."

"Rather generous, aren't you?" Fargo quipped.

"You're a lot handsomer than most, and I've always had a special fondness for good-looking galoots." The dove arched her shoulders so that her twin mounds swelled toward him like watermelons ripe enough to burst. "My name is Molly, by the way, and I get off at one. In case you'd like some company later on."

Fargo smiled. "I'll keep it in mind." Boldly reaching up, he covered her right breast and gently squeezed.

Molly blushed ever so slightly, her full cherry lips forming a delectable O. "Your hands are nice and warm," she complimented him. "Unlike some of the lunkheaded drovers who waltz through here. I'd swear they were made of ice."

Fargo could feel her nipple through the sheer fabric, the rounded tip as hard as a nail. On an impulse he flicked it with a finger and Molly wriggled in delight.

"Play your cards right and you can do that to your heart's content," she declared.

"Speaking of cards," Fargo said, reluctantly lowering his arm, "I've got to find a game to sit in on." He had come to Bob Potee's to try and recoup his losses.

Molly leaned forward. Her mouth brushed his ear, her breath fanning his neck as she whispered, "Whatever you do, stay away from the table at the back. One of the regulars there, a big gent called Guzman, is the slickest cheat this side of the Rockies. He'll fleece you dry."

"Thanks for the warning," Fargo said, patting her firm backside.

Giggling, Molly straightened. "I'll be waiting right here at one o'clock, and you better not disappoint me."

Fargo touched the tip of her chin, then blended into

the stream of new arrivals flowing into the luxurious interior. The owner, Potee, had spared no expense. Plush wine red carpet covered the floor. Mahogany paneling adorned the walls. Overhead, large chandeliers sparkled, while the room was crammed with polished tables and chairs. Up on a small but elegant stage, a balding piano player provided lively music.

At the bar customers were lined up three deep. Fargo waited his turn, ordered a whiskey, and took his drink toward the rear. Sweet little Molly didn't realize it, but her friendly advice had given him an idea.

Four men were seated at the last table. Guzman was easy to pick out. Overweight, with oily hair and flabby jowls, he wore a black frock coat, white shirt, and a string tie. For all his bulk, he handled the cards with casual ease, his thick fingers flowing with superb speed, the trademark of a true professional.

Fargo sipped his drink and observed for a spell, taking his measure of the players. One was a mousy sort who held his cards close to his vest. Another was an older man who always left his on the table after glancing at them. The third had no business playing poker. He wore his cards on his face, as it were, his expression always betraying whether he had been dealt good ones or bad.

They were playing for average stakes, each pot no higher than twenty dollars. Fargo realized he must play carefully until he had enough to make his move.

It was Guzman's turn to deal, and he did so fluidly, his fingers flying with practiced precision. If he was going to cheat, now was when he would do it.

Fargo watched closely but noticed nothing out of the ordinary—at first.

The game was draw poker. The mousy player asked for three cards, the older gent for two, while the third jasper stood pat. That left Guzman, who announced in his gravely voice, "The dealer takes one," and dealt a card to himself, shading the deal, doing it so slickly that no one other than Fargo caught on.

3

It was an old trick. Guzman started to slide off the uppermost card using his thumb. But the card wasn't halfway off when he used his second and third fingers to propel the bottom card forward in its stead. It was all done in the blink of an eye, so smoothly that it looked as if he had dealt properly. Truly flawless sleight of hand.

Fargo wasn't the least bit surprised when Guzman raised the ante from the usual dollar to two. Nor when it turned out the others had good enough cards to stay in the game, but not good enough to win the final pot, which totaled over forty dollars—twice as much as usual.

Finishing off the rest of his coffin varnish in a single gulp, Fargo pulled out an empty chair. "Mind if I sit in?" he said, sliding down before anyone could answer.

"Not at all, mister," Guzman said curtly. "So long as you don't mind parting company with your money."

The mousy player was more courteous. "Be our guest, friend. Good luck to you. I'm Harold Pinder."

Guzman snorted. "Do you think he cares who you are, you yack? All he's interested in is your cash." Guzman gave the deck to the older player. "Your turn to deal, Simmons."

The fourth man, the one whose expression always gave him away, sorted through his small amount of coins and bills. "Another couple of hands and I'll be busted again. I swear, I have the worst luck of anyone I know. If I had a lick of common sense, I'd give up this stinking game."

"Your luck isn't that rotten, Barkley," Guzman surprised Fargo by saying. "Remember that time you won pretty near sixty dollars? And last month when you almost cleaned me out until I turned the tables?"

Fargo wasn't fooled by the cardsharp's seemingly kind comments. Guzman wanted Barkley to keep coming back because poor players like him were easy to fleece. Fargo guessed that Guzman had let Barkley win so Barkley wouldn't lose interest. There was no doubt about it; the gambler was one slick hombre.

Harold Pinder adjusted his spectacles. "Tell me, friend," he addressed Fargo, "if I'm not being too nosy, what do you do for a living?"

"I've done some scouting, guided a few wagon trains," Fargo said without going into detail. His personal life was no one's business but his own.

"You don't say," Harold remarked. "I thought as much, how you're dressed and all." He gave a tiny cough. "Tell me. Are you, perhaps, in need of gainful employment? My cousin is looking for a reliable guide to take him across the prairie. Would you be interested?"

Guzman drummed his fingers on the table. "Is this a card game or a damned church social? You chatter worse than a chipmunk, Harold. You know that?"

Fargo didn't like how the cardsharp butted in. And since he had no employment prospects lined up for the immediate future, he said to Pinder, "Where do I find this cousin of yours? I'll look him up tomorrow."

"His name is Jace Carver," Harold responded. "Second cousin on my mother's side. He has his own business, Carver Supply, over on Jefferson Avenue. Can't hardly miss it, what with the huge yellow sign he has out front."

Guzman chuckled. "It's hard to believe you and Jace are kin. The two of you are as different as night from day."

"Oh, I don't know. Everyone says we have the same chin and nose," Harold said defensively. "We're not all that different."

"Neither is a mountain lion and a lamb," the gambler countered, and roared at his own wit.

Simmons began to deal. "Here we go, boys, Same as before. A pair or better to open."

Fargo played conservatively, only raising when the cards were in his favor. He learned early on that it was simple to tell when Harold and Barkley were bluffing. Harold gnawed on his lower lip, and Barkley looked

5

as if he were sitting on broken glass. Simmons was inscrutable but he never took risks, never betting more than a dollar or two no matter how good his cards were. As for Guzman, he was a master at manipulating the others, reading them as some people read a book.

By the end of an hour Fargo was seven dollars ahead. Not much, but he now had a total of twenty-five plus some odd cents. He started betting a bit more, and by the end of the second hour he was up to thirty-five.

"I told you," Barkley remarked, tapping what little was left of his pile. "I should have quit long ago."

"Stick it out," Guzman said. "Lady Luck might smile on you yet."

But she didn't. A quarter of an hour later Barkley had barely ten dollars to his name. Simmons had about twelve, Harold Pinder a bit more.

"Tell you what," Fargo said, glancing at Guzman. "Why don't we hike the stakes? Five dollars to open, and each raise must be five or more. What do you say?"

"Going for broke, eh?" Guzman said. "I'm willing if everyone else is."

Barkley shook his head and raked in what was left of his money. "Count me out, gentlemen. If I go home plumb broke again, my missus will take a rolling pin to my noggin."

Harold Pinder rubbed his hands together excitedly. "I'm staying. This is getting interesting."

Simmons shrugged. "It doesn't make no nevermind to me how high the stakes are. I'm in for the duration."

Play resumed. It was Harold's turn to deal and he did so with exquisite care, taking forever to shuffle and an eternity to deal. He counted each card aloud, slowly sliding each and every one across the table as if he were afraid they would break.

"You're about to put me to sleep," Guzman complained. "Any slower and I'd swear you were made of molasses."

"I'm being thorough," Harold defended himself.

"You're being stupid," Guzman snapped.

Fargo ended up with two kings, a queen, a ten, and a two. He debated whether to just keep the pair and finally decided to hold on to the lady, too. It was well he did. He was given another queen—and one more king. Now he had a full house. Only four of a kind, a straight flush, and a royal flush could beat it. But when it was his turn to raise, he only did so by five dollars. He didn't want to clean the table just yet, not when Guzman was due to deal next.

Fargo won the pot, a grand total of thirty dollars. Now he had more than enough to lure Guzman in. Simmons helped by folding. Harold Pinder mulled it over a bit and decided to stick in the game.

"Give me the cards," Guzman said, sweeping them in. He shuffled twice, then cut one-handed, a feat few were capable of. Shuffling twice more, he tilted the deck. Not much, but enough for him to be able to see part of the bottom card. No one noticed except Fargo. Guzman was too crafty.

"Here's where we separate the greenhorns from the longhorns," the gambler declared, bestowing a thinly disguised sneer on Fargo.

"I hope I have enough to hold out," Harold said, frowning. He was down to eleven dollars or so.

Fargo gestured. "Do yourself a favor and bow out while you can."

"What for? It's only money."

"This from someone who makes his living as an accountant," Guzman said, shaking his head. "If your clients only knew."

"I resent your insinuation, sir," Harold said stiffly. "I'd never betray their trust. I'm no swindler."

"Don't have a calf," Guzman responded. "I never said you were." As they talked, the gambler dealt, displaying his usual precise skill.

Fargo picked his cards up and fanned them. He

hadn't fared as well this time around. Fate had granted him a four of clubs, a seven of hearts, a ten of spades, a jack of hearts, and a queen of diamonds. Ordinarily he would discard the lower three and hold on to the face cards, but at the last instant he changed his mind and kept the ten of spades, hoping to draw an outside straight. Once again his hunch played out. A nine of clubs and a king of diamonds were slid across, giving him a high straight.

Harold Pinder was gnawing on his lower lip. When it came his turn, he asked for three cards and then smacked them down in irritation. "So much for recouping my losses! I should go beat my head against a wall. I fold."

That left Fargo and Guzman.

"I'll take two," the gambler said.

Pretending to be interested in his hand, Fargo peered at the cardsharp from under hooded eyelids, waiting for the crucial moment when Guzman attempted to deal from the bottom of the deck. He had to time it just right. Too soon or too late and he would be made to look the fool himself.

Then it happened. Guzman started to slide the top card outward. In the flash of an instant he did the same with the bottom card, contriving, as he had before, to slide the bottom one past the top one while simultaneously replacing the top card back.

Fargo's right hand streaked across the intervening space. His fingers clamped on to Guzman's, trapping the gambler in the act of double-dealing.

"What the hell!" Guzman bellowed, trying to jerk away.

"What's going on?" Harold asked in bewilderment.

Equally puzzled, Barkley blurted, "Here now! No grabbing allowed!"

Only Simmons caught on. Leaning forward, he pointed at the two cards wedged between Guzman's fingers. "Son of a bitch! Look there, boys! That slick bastard is trying to cheat!" Simmons shook a fist.

"How many times have you pulled that stunt on us before, you lowdown snake in the grass?"

As red as a beet, the veins on his temples bulging, Guzman heaved upward. "Let go!" he snarled, tugging to free himself.

Games at nearby tables halted. Patrons shifted in their seats to stare, those who recognized the dirty dealer, scowling at him in contempt.

Guzman stepped back and yanked harder. His hand slipped loose. In the process, he dropped cards all over his chair and the floor. Glaring balefully, he rubbed his fingers where Fargo had gripped them. "So help me, I'll blow out your wick for this!"

Simmons, Pinder, and Barkley also rose, the older man bobbing his chin at the gambler. "You're the one who should be turned into wolf bait! You rotten cheat! I have half a mind to go to Bob Potee."

"That won't be necessary," interjected a dapper man who materialized from out of the gaping onlookers, his hands on his hips, his countenance a study in indignation. "I warned you, Guzman. But you wouldn't listen."

"Now hold on, Bob—" the gambler said.

"*Silence!*" the smaller man snapped, his voice like the crack of a bullwhip. As if on cue, two burly characters in dark suits appeared at either elbow, their jackets parted to reveal the pistols they carried underneath.

Guzman was furious but he held his tongue.

"I told you there had been a few complaints," Bob Potee said crisply. "I warned you that if anyone ever proved you were a cheat, I'd have you thrown out and permanently banned." Potee crooked a finger and the two burly characters moved in closer to the fuming gambler. "My men will escort you out. Don't ever step foot on these premises again."

It was too much for Guzman. "Don't you want to hear my side?"

"No. I've been keeping my eye on you, and I happened to see the whole thing. You finally ran up against someone with quicker hands than yours."

Raw hatred blazed in the look the gambler cast at Fargo. "You've made the biggest mistake of your life, mister. You hear me? This isn't over."

Bob Potee motioned and the pair of burly bouncers each took hold of one of Guzman's arms.

"Wait a minute! What about my money?"

"*Your* money?" Potee said sarcastically. "You fleeced these others out of most of it. Besides, you know how cheating is handled. The cheat's money always goes to whoever he was playing against when he's caught. And since only you and this fellow in buckskins were still in the game, it's all his."

The glowering gambler was ushered out as Bob Potee came around the table. "A word to the wise, mister," he said to Fargo. "A coyote like Guzman isn't about to forgive and forget. He'll lie in wait and put a slug in your back the first chance he gets."

"Let him try," Fargo replied.

Potee gazed around the crowded room, and sighed. "I'm truly sorry. I try my best to run clean games, but I can't be everywhere at once. Occasionally a bad apple like Guzman crops up."

"You can't blame yourself," Fargo said, helping himself to the pot and Guzman's large pile.

"I'm the owner. Like it or not, the responsibility rests on my shoulders." Potee regarded him and the other three. "To help make it up to you, your drinks are on the house for the rest of the night. Just ask the barkeep at this end of the bar. I'll tell him to set you up."

Harold Pinder, Barkley, and Simmons exchanged grins. "That's awful nice of you, Mr. Potee," Harold said.

"Consider it a bribe," Potee said, not entirely in jest. "I don't want any of you going around saying I run a crooked gambling house."

"We'd never do that," Simmons assured him.

"Hell, no," Barkley said. "Everyone in Kansas City knows you're as honest as the year is long."

The dapper owner bid them good evening and melted into the throng.

Fargo had accumulated a small hill of coins and bills. He commenced counting it, laying the bills out in a row according to their denominations and stacking the coins by type. The grand total came to one hundred and fifty-three dollars, not quite as much as he had thought it would be, but enough to keep him in whiskey and women for another week or more. Looking up, he saw the others staring at his newfound wealth as if it were juicy steak and they hadn't eaten for a week.

"He cheated us, too," Harold Pinder remarked rather timidly.

"That he did," Fargo allowed. "But you dropped out."

"It's not fair," Barkley whined. "Guzman took a lot more of our money than he did of yours."

Simmons waved a hand in dismissal of the notion. "It doesn't matter, George. How's this guy supposed to know whose is whose? It's not like those bills have our names on them. He has a right to it all. That's just how these things go."

They went to leave.

"Hold on," Fargo said, and counted out three piles of fifteen dollars apiece. It was approximately how much each had lost since he sat down. "Help yourselves. And next time be more careful about who you play cards with."

"Thanks, stranger!" Harold beamed. "You're all right. I'll be sure to tell my cousin about you." Stuffing the bills into a pocket, he bustled away.

Simmons took his without a word, nodded gratefully, and headed for the bar.

That left Barkley, who didn't know when he was well off. Hefting his share, he commented, "I should receive more than they did since I lost twice as much."

Fargo doubted it. "Fifteen is all you're getting. Unless you'd rather not have that." The Trailsman held out his hand, palm up.

"No, no, don't get me wrong," Barkley said hastily. "This will do just fine." But his face put the lie to his words. Clenching his fists, his spine as rigid as a board, he departed in a huff.

Since there were too many coins to tote around, Fargo took them to the cashier and exchanged them for bills. Then, never one to pass up a free drink or three, he visited the bar. A clock on the wall revealed it was a few minutes shy of midnight. Another hour, yet, before Molly was done for the night.

A familiar figure stepped to his side. "Simmons just mentioned what you did, mister. Damned decent of you."

"Barkley didn't think so."

Bob Potee snickered. "Some people are so soured on life, they can't get the acid out of their systems. And he's one of them." Potee offered his hand. "I don't believe I caught your name."

Shaking hands, Fargo told him.

The proprietor's thin eyebrows arched. "Do tell. Your reputation precedes you, Trailsman. Had I known who you were, I wouldn't have butted in earlier. I'd have let Guzman go for his gun so the undertaker could plant him six feet under tomorrow." Potee scanned the boisterous throng. "On second thought, the last thing I'd want in here is a gunfight. Too many bystanders. I'd better have one of my boys stand guard out front in case Guzman tries to sneak back in to get his revenge."

"Tell you what." Fargo had an inspiration. "I'll do you a favor and leave, if you'll do me a favor in return."

"Name it."

Fargo did.

Bob Potee grinned from ear to ear. "Consider it done. But keep in mind that when Guzman cuts loose, anyone near you could take a slug. And I wouldn't want her hurt. She's a mighty sweet filly."

"Me either." Fargo thanked him and ambled to the long hall. Molly was still there, still smiling and flirting and parading her bosom as if it had won first place at the county fair. She didn't see him come up behind her, and she jumped when his arm looped around her waist.

"Time to go, gorgeous," Fargo said and pecked her on the neck.

"Are you drunk?" Molly responded, giggling. "I don't get off until one, remember? You'll have to wait a while yet, handsome."

"Potee gave his permission for you to leave early." The warmth of her body and the musky fragrance of her perfume combined to cause a twitching in Fargo, low down. He swung her around so they faced one another, her ample breasts cushioned against his broad chest. "Your place? Or my hotel room?"

Molly traced the outline of his jaw, a playful twinkle animating her eyes. "My, my. What *do* you have in mind?"

"Let's put it this way. Potee also gave you tomorrow off, with pay." Fargo steered her through the gilded double doors and started down a flight of carpeted stairs. He wasn't unduly worried about Guzman. If trouble came, he expected it to be outside, and he would be ready for it.

But no sooner did they reach the bottom than a bellowed curse rent the air, punctuated by blasts of gunfire.

2

The building at number 3 Missouri Avenue was divided in half. Upstairs was Potee's gambling hall, famed throughout the city. Equally famous, and just as lavish, was the fine restaurant that occupied the ground floor. Both stayed open until near dawn. Both did a thriving business.

So it was that when Skye Fargo and Molly came to the bottom of the stairs, the corridor ahead contained close to a dozen people. The restaurant was on their left. Fifty feet away was the main entrance, and framed in it was the livid figure of Guzman holding a smoking Smith & Wesson.

His first two shots missed, but not by much. Fargo heard them buzz by his ears like riled bees. As Guzman took aim to try again, Fargo's hand dipped to his Colt, his thumb curling around the hammer and cocking it even as he cleared leather. He fired from the hip, a snap shot that sent slivers from the jamb inches from the gambler's head.

Guzman flung himself backward, then pivoted and ran.

Women were screaming, men shouting. No one sought to interfere as Fargo barreled down the corridor, yelling over his shoulder to Molly, "Stay put! I'll be back for you!" Sprinting to the entrance, he stopped and peered out.

Down the benighted street, the Smith & Wesson cracked, the bullet biting into the outer wall.

Fargo fired at the flash but couldn't tell if he scored

14

or not. Tucking at the waist, he hurtled outside and raced in pursuit.

Despite the late hour, Missouri Avenue was packed with pedestrians, carriages, and buggies. Kansas City was notorious for its rowdy nightlife, for indulging vices of every stripe from dusk until dawn.

Fargo glimpsed a bobbing shape as it rounded a corner on the fly. He skirted a group of women in lacy dresses, who were too shocked to move out of his way, then sped flat out for twenty yards. Again he paused. Again it saved his life. As he bent to peer around the corner, the Smith & Wesson banged. A slug thudded into the stone wall beside him, and he winced as sharp shards struck his cheek.

Fargo glanced at the top of the wall. It was only six feet high. Crouching, he leaped straight up, hooked his elbows over the wall, and swung his legs up. Rising into a crouch, he scoured the side street and spotted his quarry.

Guzman was in a shadowed doorway, the Smith & Wesson extended, waiting for him to come around the corner.

Fargo took deliberate aim. But at the very moment he was to squeeze the trigger, a clattering brougham passed the doorway. Inside were several men and women, singing a bawdy song. It only took a few seconds for the brougham to go by, but when it did, the doorway was empty.

"Damn!" Fargo swore under his breath, and searched anew for the cardsharp. He didn't see Guzman anywhere. Puzzled, Fargo wondered if the gambler had ducked into a building. No other explanation was possible, unless . . .

Insight swiveled Fargo toward the brougham, which was almost abreast of him. Through the window he saw the singers, young merrymakers out celebrating a night on the town. On a high seat in front sat the driver, attired in a starched uniform and high silk hat. He was gazing off to his right, at the far side of the brougham.

Fargo took two long strides and leaped. Landing lightly on the balls of his feet, he dipped at the knees so he could see under the conveyance. Sure enough, a pair of legs were pacing it, striding briskly.

Slanting toward the rear, Fargo leveled the Colt. He thought he had the gambler dead to rights, but when he bounded to the other side, no one was there. The driver cleared his throat, and when Fargo looked at him, the man pointed at an alley they had just passed.

Thanking the driver with a wave, Fargo darted over to the alleyway without delay. In his eagerness to catch Guzman he stepped into the alley mouth, and at the other end fireflies sparkled. But these were deafening fireflies, whose echoes rolled off across Kansas City like breakers rolling onto shore. Fargo answered in kind, throwing lead three times before ducking back to reload.

Another blast testified that Guzman was still alive.

Heedless of the commotion the gun battle was creating, Fargo finished replacing the spent cartridges and swung around on the balls of his feet, ready to fan the Colt. He was just in time to catch sight of the gambler speeding around the far corner.

Plunging into the alley's murky confines, Fargo flew to the next street. Throwing caution aside, he loped into the open and nearly collided with a pair of ladies strolling arm in arm. Fargo looked in the direction Guzman had gone but there was no sign of him.

A shrill whistle sounded in the distance. Another answered farther off. Their significance wasn't lost on him. Recently, Kansas City had acquired a small but efficient police force patterned after that of New York and other major cities in the East, policemen who signaled one another using whistles.

Fargo had no desire to be hauled in for hours of questioning, or to be dragged before a judge for disturbing the peace and discharging a firearm in the city limits. Twirling the Colt into its holster, he hurriedly retraced his steps.

A fair crowd had gathered in front of the restaurant

and a few people pointed at him but no one tried to stop him as Fargo shouldered on through and into the corridor.

Molly was gone.

Although he was disappointed, Fargo couldn't blame her. Not when she had nearly had her head blown off. He shifted to get out of there, stopping short when a warm hand brushed his neck and a sultry voice husked in his ear.

"I'd about given up hope, stranger," she whispered. "Bob Potee was just down here and told me what you did to Guzman. I was worried sick you'd been shot."

Fargo turned. "I'm fine. A little tense, is all."

The dove melted against him, soft and yielding in all the right places, her red lips tantalizingly near his own. Grinning impishly, she said, "Is that so? Take me home and I'll help you relax. Everyone says I give the best back rubs since Cleopatra."

"She gave back rubs?" Fargo joked.

"How the hell should I know?" Molly rejoined, and kissed him full on the mouth. "Now what say we skedaddle? My apartment isn't far, and it's a hell of a lot cozier than any hotel room, if I do say so myself."

"You're on." Taking her elbow, Fargo swiftly bore westward once they were outdoors.

"Hold on," Molly said. "My place is the other way."

"We'll go around the block," Fargo proposed, a precaution on his part to avoid a policeman fast approaching from the east.

"Whatever you want, handsome," Molly bantered, snuggling against him and resting her cheek on his shoulder.

Fargo stuck to the shadows. Not out of concern for the officers of the law, but in the conviction that Guzman hadn't given up, and that the gambler would try again, perhaps even stalking them at that very moment. Fargo repeatedly checked behind him but saw nothing to indicate they were being trailed.

Molly couldn't help noticing. "Keep that up and I'm the one who will need a back rub. Quit fretting! That

17

polecat isn't about to buck you twice, not after you scared him off like you did."

They made a circuit of the block. Three policemen were now in front of 3 Missouri Avenue, talking to witnesses.

Averting his face, Fargo pulled his hat brim low and quickened their pace. He half expected a shout to ring out or a whistle to blow, but none did. They walked for a good ten minutes to a residential section where few people were abroad and carriage traffic was extremely light.

Molly didn't talk his ear off, as some would. She was content to give directions, her finger constantly curling in his hair or stroking his ear. She halted at a wrought-iron gate and announced, "This is it."

Beyond reared a French-style house complete with a flower garden and a gazebo.

"I rent upstairs rooms from the sweetest old lady," Molly said fondly. "She treats me more like a daughter than a tenant." Opening the gate, she added, "I had to fib to her about what I do for a living. Agatha is very prim and proper."

All the lights in the house were out, and for all Fargo knew, the old woman was a light sleeper. "What if she hears us?"

"She won't. Agatha could sleep through a war." Molly led him around back to a flight of white wooden steps. "Watch the fourth one up. It's cracked and she hasn't gotten around to having it fixed."

They climbed upward, Molly holding on to Fargo's hand. From the landing they enjoyed a panoramic vista of the city of Kansas, aglow with hundreds of lanterns and lamps. Off to the west, the lights of a riverboat plied the broad Missouri. The faint rattle of carriages and the occasional howls of dogs wafted on the stiff breeze.

Molly inhaled deeply, and smiled. "I love it at night. Everything is so calm, so peaceful. After putting up with rowdy drunks and icy hands for eight hours, I

18

like to come home and just stand here awhile. All my cares fade away."

Fargo was more interested in the contours of her bosom, silhouetted against the glow of a streetlamp the next block over. Stepping around behind her, he wrapped both arms around her waist and nuzzled the nape of her neck.

"Now, now," Molly chided. "Enough of that. Not out here. Wait until we're inside."

"Why? You said your landlord sleeps like a log," Fargo reminded her, licking the smooth skin above the collar of her dress.

Molly arched her back, her sculpted posterior pressing back against his manhood. "I'm very sensitive there. You're making me tingle all over."

"That's the general idea," Fargo teased, licking her ear and then fastening his lips to her earlobe.

Squirming deliciously, Molly placed both hands on his forearms and sighed. "Mmmm. I'm even more sensitive there. Keep that up and you'll have a wildcat on your hands."

"Promises, promises," Fargo said. He sucked on her lobe, then rimmed it with tiny nibbles that caused the brunette to shiver as if she were cold.

"Ohhh. I knew you would be good. I just knew it."

"Did you really?" Fargo slid his hands up over her shapely hips, across her flat stomach, to her breasts. She gasped as he cupped them, then groaned when he squeezed.

"Believe it or not, I'm sensitive there, too," Molly huskily mentioned, wearing a wide grin.

"Is there anywhere you're *not* sensitive?" Fargo said, and suddenly pinched her nipples through her sheer red dress.

"Yes, yes!" Molly breathed, her lovely face upturned to the stars, her ripe mouth parted, her eyes closed.

Fargo's pole surged to attention. Placing a hand on her arm, he slowly turned her around and they embraced, gluing their hot bodies to one another, his mouth covering hers, her silken tongue darting out to probe, explore, and entwine with his. Electric sensations spread through his body as a powerful hunger grew inside of him.

Molly's lips were exquisitely soft, like miniature velvet pillows, her tongue as tasty as strawberries. Fargo sucked on it, eliciting a low moan of carnal pleasure from Molly.

They kissed for the longest while, oblivious to the world around them, lost in one another, adrift in their mutual pleasure.

It was Molly who pulled back, flushed and breathing heavily, her bosom rising and falling like a blacksmith's bellows. "Let's get inside where we can be more comfortable."

Fargo had no argument with that. He waited while she rummaged in her handbag and produced a key. A few houses down, a chain rattled and a dog began to bark in a frenzy. Fargo saw the animal but couldn't see what it was barking at. After half a minute it stopped.

Light spilled across him from indoors. A hand fell on his shoulder.

"Have you lost interest already?" Molly taunted. "I thought you had more fire in your veins."

"I'll show you fire," Fargo growled, sweeping her into his arms and carrying her over the threshold. Pushing the door shut with his foot, he walked to the middle of a modest sitting room dominated by a lavender settee. Two doorways were straight ahead, another to the right. "Which is the bedroom?" he asked.

"Guess," Molly said, tittering.

Since the lingering scent of coffee and food came from one of the rooms straight ahead, Fargo opted for the doorway to the right. A rectangle of light bathed a wide canopy bed rimmed at the headboard by huge, fluffy pillows.

"You like it?" Molly said, grinning.

"Sure do." Fargo gently laid her down and sat beside her to drink in the ravishing splendor of her magnificent body. Her luxurious hair glinted like a halo, her heaving mounds were thrust upward, and her dress clung to her thighs in an enticing invitation. A lump formed in his throat, while his pants bulged.

Molly chuckled. "What's the matter? Having second thoughts?"

"You talk too much," Fargo replied, lowering his lips to hers. Their kiss was fiery, their passion rising by leaps and bounds. Fargo roved his hands over her shoulders, her breasts, and her hips. She did likewise, her fingers dancing brazenly near his manhood.

Removing his hat, gunbelt, and boots, Fargo put them on the floor.

Molly took off his buckskin shirt herself, rolled it up, and threw it over by the wall. Sitting up with a new gleam in her eyes, she reached for his pants. "Mercy me, look at the size of you!" she cooed. Unhitching them, she pushed them down around his knees, then wrapped her fingers around his member and bent forward.

An involuntary groan escaped Fargo. He placed his hands on her head and fought an impulse to prematurely explode. Her gliding tongue gradually incited him to a feverish pitch, and when she treated him as if he were hard candy, it was all he could do to control himself. How long she dallied, he couldn't say. But at last she straightened and he eased her on to her back.

Undoing the buttons and fasteners, Fargo pulled her dress off, exposing her huge breasts, her marble legs, all of her full, wonderful beauty. Her nipples jutted at him like twin mountain peaks. Swooping to her right one, he sucked and pulled, prompting a gurgling whine. When he shifted his attention to the other breast, her legs parted and rose to wrap around his hips.

Fargo delved lower, sliding his fingers up over her knee, along her glassy thigh, to her nether mound. Molly uttered a mewling cry as his forefinger slid across her moist slit. He found her swollen knob and rubbed.

"Ah! Ah! Oh, my!"

Kneeling, Fargo angled his mouth to where his finger had just been. At the first contact, Molly bucked upward, her arms flinging outward.

"Yesssssssssssss!"

Her sweet aroma washed over Fargo as he licked and sucked and flicked. When his tongue lanced up into her sugary tunnel, Molly clamped her legs around his head and seized his hair as if to pull him up inside of her. She moaned nonstop now, tossing and turning, her eyes closed, lost in sensual delirium. After a bit she started to grind herself against him, harder and harder, faster and faster. Sensing how close she was, Fargo locked his lips on her knob and sucked as if it were a straw.

"Oh! I'm there, handsome! I'm theeerrre!"

That she was. She husked and panted and huffed, over the brink, mashing herself against him until she collapsed, limp and spent.

"That was nice," Molly whispered.

"We're not done yet," Fargo said. "Not by a long shot." Moving up over her so they were chest to chest, he kissed her mouth hungrily. Her fingers stroked his neck, his shoulders. In no rush, Fargo lathered her throat and her upper arms. Then he rose on his knees, held his pole, and brushed it across her moist opening.

Trembling from raw lust, Molly gazed at him in eager anticipation. "Stick it in. Please. I'm ready."

Fargo wasn't. Not when he could increase her desire, and her pleasure, tenfold. He continued to rub himself up and down, now and then inserting himself a fraction or two, but never entering, never sheathing his sword completely. The strategy worked.

Molly wheezed noisily, her hips rocking, her hands pulling at him in a vain bid to hurry him along. Her need was such that she begged him to take her, pleaded with him to bury himself inside of her. "I can't take much more of this!" she protested. "I need you inside me!"

Fargo took her at her word. Holding Molly by the

hips, he speared into her to the hilt, practically lifting her off the quilt. She threw back her head, mouth agape as if to scream, although no sounds came out. The whites of her eyes showed, and her fingernails bit deep into his arms. For long seconds they were perfectly still, then Fargo drew partly back and pumped up into her again, settling into a regular rhythm.

The bed seemed to ripple under them like waves on an ocean. Fargo paced himself, in and almost out, in and almost out. When he had an urge to go faster, he suppressed it. Not quite yet, he told himself. Not until the brunette was at the pinnacle of yearning.

Molly clung to him, her cheek against his chest, her arms wrapped tight. She matched his thrusts with thrusts of her own, matching his pace, his ardor. She bit him. Her nails drew blood from his shoulder blades.

Fargo's patience paid off.

Presently, Molly thrashed from side to side in the throes of ecstasy, her inner walls contracting around his driving pole. "Oh! Oh! Again! I'm coming again!" With that, she erupted like a geyser.

Her release triggered Fargo's. He felt a constriction in his throat and felt another much lower down. Gritting his teeth, he held out for as long as he could while she heaved under him in volcanic rapture. But there was no withstanding the inevitable.

A key of gunpowder went off in Fargo's groin. A surge of total bliss coursed through him and he groaned long and loud. Tiny pinpoints of lights danced before his eyes as his whole being was immersed in a molten flow of supreme delight. Their two bodies fused as one, pumping without cease, her cries mingling with his. All else ceased to exist. The bed, the room, the walls—everything faded into emptiness.

Fargo crested the summit and sank onto Molly, his weight cushioned by her ample melons. His pulse began to slow, as did the pounding in his temples. Like a kite sinking from the sky, he coasted down to earth.

Her hot breath fluttered in his ear, her hands were limp on his back. "You . . ." Molly said, having to lick her lips and gasp for breath. "You were sensational."

Fargo could hear her heart hammering, hear the flutter of her breath. He caressed her, then closed his eyes and was still, overcome by lethargy. All he wanted now was to sleep.

"And you convinced Bob to give me the day off tomorrow so we can spend it together?" Molly said, laughing. "Lordy, something tells me I'll be worn to a frazzle before you're done."

Fargo let himself drift into dreamland. For the first time since his clash with the gambler, he was at ease. Toward dawn he would wake up and arouse Molly again. There was no better way to start off a new day than by making love.

Suddenly Fargo was aware of a hand on his shoulder, of being shaken, of a whisper in his left ear.

"Wake up, damn it! I hard something!"

Sluggishly raising his head, Fargo blinked in confusion at the brunette's frightened features. "What?"

"I heard something!" Molly exclaimed in a low voice. "Footsteps, on the stairs, I think. Someone is out there."

"At this time of night?" Fargo wasn't sure how long he had been asleep but it couldn't have been long. Shaking his head to clear it, he eased off her and began to dress. "Maybe it's one of your gentleman callers."

Molly sat up. "I hardly ever bring anyone home. You're the first in a coon's age." Clutching her dress, she covered herself. "There! Listen!"

Fargo heard it, too, the unmistakable creak of a board, one of the steps leading up to her apartment. It galvanized him into swiftly pulling on his pants and gunbelt. Palming the Colt, he glided to the right of the bedroom doorway, out of the rectangle of light.

"Do you see anything?" Molly whispered.

Nothing moved anywhere in Fargo's range of vision except for the flickering flame of the lamp on the end

24

table next to the settee. The landing was visible through a window, but it was empty. Or so it appeared.

"Well, do you?" Molly persisted.

"No." Fargo cocked his revolver. For the life of him, he couldn't recollect if he'd locked the outer door when they came in, but he didn't think he had. To reach it, he had to cross the sitting room and could easily be picked off by whoever was out there. Tensing, he glanced at Molly. "Do you have a gun?"

"A derringer. It's in my dresser."

"Get it out in case your visitor is who I think it is. Then close this door behind me and stand over in the far corner."

Molly stayed where she was. "The derringer wouldn't do me any good. I don't have any bullets. I used them all up when I killed a rat in the basement last winter."

How many shots could it take to kill a rat? Fargo wondered. And as if she could read his thoughts, she elaborated.

"Agatha spotted it and started screaming. The thing was running all over the place, behind boxes, up in the beams, back behind the washbasin. I fired twenty-seven times before I finally hit it in the leg. We finished it off with a broom." Molly paused. "I guess I'm not exactly the best shot in the world."

"Not anywhere close," Fargo whispered, then focused on the front window as a shadow flitted across it. Crouching, he darted to a rocking chair, then proceeded on behind the settee and along it to the end table. Taking hold of the lamp, he pulled it toward him and blew out the wick, plunging the sitting room into darkness.

"Skye?" Molly called out.

Fargo didn't answer, not when the lurker outside might hear him and peg his position. Pushing the lamp back, he inched around the table far enough to see the window clearly. A vague shape moved, not more than a suggestion of size and bulk. It was a man, a big man. Guzman, Fargo reckoned.

"Skye!" Molly stood in the bedroom doorway, her dress clasped in front of her. "Where are you?"

Annoyed she hadn't done as he'd instructed her, and even more peeved at how recklessly she had exposed herself, Fargo risked giving himself away by whispering, "Get back in there, damn it! And close the door!"

Molly stamped her foot in anger, then obeyed. Only she didn't just close it, she *slammed* it, loud enough to be heard at Bob Potee's place.

Fargo moved warily forward. What with the lamp being extinguished and Molly's little tantrum, stealth was no longer critical. Whoever was out there knew they were on to him. But he wasn't about to invite a slug.

Reaching the window, Fargo glanced over the bottom sill. No one was on the landing. Slowly rising higher, he was mystified to discover no one was on the stairs, either. Yet that couldn't be. He was positive someone had been there moments ago.

Twisting the latch, Fargo edged the door wide enough for him to slip out. With every nerve jangling, he crab-stepped to the railing. The yard below lay serene and undisturbed under the starlight.

Maybe he had been wrong, Fargo told himself. Maybe his eyes had deceived him. But then, what about the creaking sounds?

As if in response, there was another creak. Only this one was *above* him. Twisting, Fargo glanced up just as a darkling form sprang at him from the edge of the roof.

3

Skye Fargo had no chance to react. His reflexes were second to none but his attacker slammed into him before he could squeeze off a shot. It felt as if he had been smashed into by a ten-ton boulder, the impact jolting him against the rail, which snapped with a sharp crack. For several moments Fargo tilted precariously backward, on the verge of pitching over. Only the attacker's iron fingers, clamped around his throat and wrist, kept him from falling.

As Fargo had suspected, it was Guzman. The gambler's face was contorted in feral ferocity, bloodlust glinting in his eyes. Guzman hissed like a viper as he sought to constrict his fingers tighter around Fargo's neck while simultaneously holding the Trailsman's gun arm at bay. "I warned you!" he raged. "Now you die!"

Fargo tried to throw the gambler off but couldn't brace his legs sufficiently. Although Fargo was taller, the gambler had a good sixty- to seventy-pound weight advantage.

Fargo couldn't manage to pry off the fingers at his throat. They were rigid as steel bands, and sinking in steadily deeper by the second. Fargo attempted to level the Colt but was thwarted. That left him one recourse. Streaking his left hand down low, he balled his fist and drove it into Guzman's groin, twice in swift succession. Unless the gambler was a eunuch, the blows were bound to have an effect.

And they did.

Sputtering in fury, Guzman doubled over, his grip slackening as he sucked in air. "Bastard!" he spat.

Seizing the initiative, Fargo uncoiled. With a sudden wrench, he threw Guzman off, but the gambler only stumbled back a couple of feet. As Fargo extended the Colt, Guzman leaped in close again, gripping his forearm to prevent him from shooting.

Locked together, they grappled, Fargo striving to bring the Colt into play and the gambler doing all in his power to hinder him. They churned to the right, then to the left. They spun completely around, bumping off rails and the wall.

Fargo lost all track of where he was in relation to the doorway and the stairs, but he found out a moment later when Guzman lost his balance and lurched wildly. They were directly above the steps!

Gravity took hold of Guzman, and the cardsharp started to slip backward. He held on to Fargo in desperation while scrambling to regain his balance, but instead of stopping himself from falling he pulled Fargo down on top of him and they both toppled, tumbling head over heels.

Fargo was bounced, jarred, bumped, and bruised. He grabbed at the rails in vain but couldn't find purchase. Halfway down, the Colt went flying. In an ungainly swirl of arms and legs he came to a stop on the second step, flat on his back with his body bent at an unnatural angle.

There was no time to catch his breath. Guzman had landed in the grass and was already rising, snorting like a bull about to charge.

Shifting around, scraping his shins and temple, Fargo pushed up into a crouch. He leaped just as the gambler rushed toward him, tackling Guzman around the waist. Down they went, but compared to the hard stairs, the grass was as soft as Molly's quilt.

Fargo lashed out, his right fist connecting with Guzman's jaw. In retaliation, the gambler punched him in the gut. They rolled apart and rose. Guzman seemed a bit unsteady, but he immediately recovered.

"I could have shot you when you stepped outside. That would be too easy, though. I want the satisfaction of killing you with my bare hands—or with this." The gambler's hand disappeared under his frock coat, then whipped out, holding a bone-handled knife with a blade over seven inches long.

Fargo skipped aside as the cold steel snaked at his throat. He dodged another lunge, then backpedaled to gain room to maneuver. Bending, he slid his Arkansas toothpick from the sheath strapped to his right ankle.

Guzman rushed forward but instantly retreated when the slender toothpick arced up and out, nearly opening his cheek. Cautious now, Guzman hefted his weapon and circled to the left. "So you have a knife, too. It won't help you—nothing will. I've been in more knife fights than any man in Kansas City. And I always win."

"Prove it," Fargo challenged.

Growling like a rabid wolf, Guzman pressed his assault. Slashing, stabbing, cutting from every angle, he attempted to make good on his boast.

Fargo was hard-pressed to defend himself. He parried, blocked, weaved, and danced, always a heartbeat ahead of razor-sharp steel. Guzman demonstrated the same quickness with the bone-handled knife that he had with cards. Fargo couldn't deny the man was skilled—maybe one of the most skilled knife fighters he had ever gone up against.

They fought largely in silence, except for the ring of their blades and the shuffle of their feet. Guzman cursed when Fargo nicked his forearm, and again when Fargo feinted with the toothpick and delivered a vicious kick to the gambler's left leg.

Suddenly the lawn was bathed in a rosy glow.

Startled, Guzman sprang back out of reach and glanced up.

So did Fargo. To his consternation, he saw Molly on the landing, dressed in a robe. In one hand she held the relit lamp aloft, in the other she had her useless derringer.

But the gambler didn't know it was useless. Spinning, he raced toward the gate, spitting venomously over his shoulder, "Damn your little bitch! But don't worry. I keep my promises! And next time, there won't be anyone around to bail you out!"

Fargo gave chase, intent on ending it. Fleeter than Guzman, he rapidly overtook him and was only a few yards behind when Fargo's bare right foot came down hard on a jagged object in the grass. What it was, he couldn't say, but pain spiked through him and he tripped and nearly fell. Limping badly in torment, he hobbled to a halt and had to watch in helpless anger as Guzman sped out through the gate and off down the street.

Hunkering down, Fargo examined his foot. There was no heavy flow of blood, but there was a small gash where something, a rock, maybe, had ripped into his flesh.

"Skye? Are you all right?"

Fargo frowned in disapproval at the brunette as she hurried up. "I told you to stay in the bedroom."

"I'm sorry. I couldn't. I was too worried."

The sincerity in her tone touched him. Fargo couldn't stay mad. Draping his arm across her shoulders, he said, "You're sweet, but you could have been hurt if he was using a gun instead of a knife."

Molly swung the lamp from side to side. "That *was* Guzman, wasn't it? I didn't get a good look at his face. Where is he? Did he get away?"

"I'm afraid so." Fargo knew he had to be on his guard every minute, never knowing when the gambler might strike.

"He must have followed us from Potee's," Molly said.

"Tomorrow we're buying you a box of ammunition," Fargo advised. "You're to carry that derringer with you at all times." Not that he figured Guzman would try to harm her. It was more a case of being safe than sorry.

"He won't give up, will he?"

"Not this side of the grave, no." Fargo had encountered revenge-driven cutthroats like Guzman before, hard cases who wouldn't rest until any wrong done them was erased by shedding the blood of the party responsible.

"Maybe you should go to the police," Molly suggested.

Fargo shook his head. Some things a man had to do for himself. Not out of any false pride or silly stubbornness, but as a measure of his worth *as* a man. Grit and backbone weren't just words in a dictionary. Courage wasn't some fancy highbrow concept. Any man who wanted to be able to look himself in the mirror had to stand up for himself and demonstrate those qualities when put to the test. It would be a sorry day indeed if things reached the point where people ran bawling to the law like babes to their mamas every time someone glanced at them crosswise.

"Then find out where he hangs his hat and pay him a visit," Molly said.

Fargo intended to do just that. The only person he knew of who might be able to help, though, was Bob Potee. "What time does your boss usually show up at the gambling hall?"

"About four in the afternoon. Why?"

"Is there anyone else who might be able to tell me where Guzman lives?"

"Not that I can think of, offhand. Maybe one of the barkeeps. Or some of the other gamblers. He tends to keep pretty much to himself."

After retrieving the Colt, they went back upstairs. Fargo made a point of bolting her door this time.

Refusing to take no for an answer, Molly shooed him to the kitchen and insisted on pouring him a glass of red-eye, which did wonders to reduce the aches from his many bruises and bumps. They sat and talked awhile, Molly relating the story of how she had wound up working for Bob Potee. Her tale was familiar. Once she had been happily married with two small children. Then calamity struck and she lost her husband when a tree he was sawing down in order to clear ground for their new homestead fell the wrong way, crushing him.

Left on her own with two mouths to feed, Molly desperately sought work. But jobs for women were scarce, jobs that paid well even scarcer. Potee, however, paid extremely well. So she had gone to work for him. But five months later, she lost both her daughters to a fever that tore through the city, claiming scores of lives.

"Now I just live from day to day, not really caring about anything other than getting by," Molly concluded her account.

"You should remarry," Fargo said. Some soiled doves weren't meant to be hitched, but Molly plainly was. Her face had shone with happiness when she talked about her husband and children.

"Are you loco? I'm used goods. What man would have me?"

"Any man with half a brain. You're a fine woman, Molly. And you're young enough yet that you could start another family if you wanted."

She cocked her head. "You're sure a strange one, handsome. Most men would rather I part my legs for money the rest of my born days."

"Who cares what anyone else wants?" Fargo responded. "It's what you want to do with your own life that counts."

"I know. But it's hard sometimes to pick up the pieces after our lives go sour on us."

On that note Fargo rose and stretched. "Time to turn in. I'll sleep on the settee in case Guzman pays us a return visit."

"Like hell you will," Molly responded. "He's not stupid enough to try and break in. And I want you by my side in bed."

Fargo grinned. "I never argue with a lady." He paused. "Well, almost never." He hadn't realized quite how tired he was until they were under the covers, her head resting on his chest. A torrent of fatigue gushed through him, oozing from every pore and rendering his eyelids as heavy as lead. He dozed off thinking of Molly's breasts, and how he couldn't wait to give them the attention they deserved come morning.

Out of habit, Fargo woke up at the crack of dawn. A growing glow framed the bedroom window, and a legion of birds were warbling and chirping in an avian chorus. He felt refreshed, but stiff and sore. Molly slumbered away, angelic in repose, as he drank in her beauty, reluctant to wake her up just yet.

But Molly was awakened anyway—by the clomp of heavy shoes on the stairs.

Fargo sat up, nearly spilling her off the bed. From the sound of things there was more than one visitor. Sliding out from under the covers, he donned his pants and boots and shucked the Colt from its holster, which he had hung over the bedpost the night before.

"Guzman, you reckon?" Molly anxiously asked, blinking sleep away.

"Making that much noise? And in broad daylight?" Fargo moved past the bed. "This time do as I tell you and stay in here."

As he strode into the front room Fargo saw two men in suits and bowlers step onto the landing. One had short black hair and a mustache, the other a hawkish nose and a jutting jaw. The one with the mustache politely knocked.

Fargo worked the bolt and pulled the door wide in case it was a ruse and they planned to jump him. But both stood there, smiling thinly.

"Good morning, sir," the one with the mustache said. "My name is Oliver Meachum. This other gentleman is Carl Banner."

"What do you want?" Fargo asked a shade gruffly.

"We're sorry to disturb you so early, sir," Meachum said, "but our employer sent us to fetch you. He would appreciate it if you would see fit to join him for breakfast."

"Me?" Fargo couldn't think of anyone who would go to so much bother.

Carl Banner answered. "You *are* Skye Fargo? And you did play cards with Harold Pinder last night?"

Fargo recalled the mousy little poker player. "Yes, but—"

"Since Harold Pinder didn't know your name, our employer wisely thought Bob Potee might," Banner said. "We paid him a visit late last night."

Meachum continued. "Mr. Potee mentioned how you had left his establishment with the young lady who lives at this address, so here we are."

"Now if you'll finish dressing, sir," Banner said, "we'll escort you to our employer. A carriage is waiting out front."

"Not so damn fast," Fargo said, galled that they took it for granted that he would go along with no questions asked. "Who is this employer you keep talking about?"

"Why, Jace Carver, sir," Banner stated as if that explained everything.

"Why does he want to see me?"

Meachum and Banner swapped looks. "Do you mean to say you didn't offer to act in the capacity of Mr. Carver's guide?" the former inquired.

"Guide?" Fargo responded, puzzled. Then he remembered. Harold Pinder had said something about having a cousin who needed one. But what with Guzman trying to kill him and Molly's charming company, he had forgotten all about it.

"Are we to infer Mr. Pinder was mistaken?" Banner said. "He informed Mr. Carver that you planned to pay him a visit today, and our employer graciously thought he would save you the trouble of looking him up."

"This early?"

Both men smiled.

"Mr. Carver isn't one to let grass grow underneath him, sir," Meachum said. "When he wants something done, he does it. He's quite motivated in that regard."

"But not excessively so," Banner amended.

Something about the way they constantly praised

34

the virtues of their boss struck Fargo as downright peculiar. Still, Carver had gone to a lot of trouble to meet him, so the least he could do was agree. What harm could it do? "Give me five minutes."

"Take as long as you need," Meachum replied. "We're not going anywhere."

"Not without you," Banner added.

Irritated by their smug attitude, Fargo closed the door and bolted it. Turning, he saw Molly in the bedroom doorway, the quilt draped over her slender shoulders. "You couldn't listen if your life depended on it, could you?"

"I just wanted to make sure you weren't in any trouble." She peered out the window. "Who are those two "

"A man by the name of Jace Carver sent them. I need to go, but I won't be long." Fargo brushed by her and over to where his shirt lay.

"You know Jace Carver? I'm impressed."

"Who is he?"

"Only one of the richest and most powerful men in the whole territory, is all." Molly leaned against the jamb and the quilt slipped down over her arm, baring part of her full breast. "He sells stuff to just about everybody. To the army, to the trading posts along the frontier, every dry-goods store in the city. Folks say he's got more money than old King Midas."

Welcome news, Fargo reflected. If Jace Carver was so wealthy, he could afford to pay top dollar.

"I saw him once," Molly mentioned. "At Potee's. He had a woman on each arm and no less than six personal guards." She pulled the quilt back up. "He's not someone you want to take lightly. Rumor has it he's got a mean streak a mile wide."

"I'll keep that in mind." Fargo had shrugged into his shirt and now strapped on his gunbelt.

Molly winked at him. "Don't take too long, you hear? I was looking forward to cuddling with you awhile."

"I'll keep that in mind," Fargo repeated, smirking.

Fully dressed, he walked over and passionately kissed her. "That should tide you over until I get back."

"Almost. But to be sure—" Molly threw her arms around him and fused her mouth to his. When they finally pulled apart minutes later, she leaned back, deliberately allowing the quilt to fall again, only a lot further. "Just so you'll remember what you're coming back to," she teased.

Laughing, Fargo ambled out, saying, "Bolt the door behind me. And don't let anyone in you don't know."

"Yes, master," Molly said, and chortled.

Meachum and Banner were still waiting. Neither criticized him for taking so long or bothered to inquire about the shattered rail.

"After you, sir," Meachum said.

The sun was perched on the eastern horizon but an invigorating chill lingered in the air, and Fargo breathed deep as he strolled toward the wrought-iron gate. He scanned the grass for the object he had stepped on the night before but didn't see anything. When he looked up, he almost stopped cold in amazement.

The carriage at the curb wasn't just any carriage. It was the longest, the widest, the fanciest, most luxurious carriage Fargo had ever set eyes on, and that said a lot. Six magnificent white horses were in harness, and not one but *two* coachmen wearing bright yellow uniforms sat on the leather-upholstered driver's box, both wearing high silk hats and yellow gloves. One held a thin whip.

"Impressive, isn't it?" Meachum said. "Mr. Carver had it custom-made in Philadelphia and shipped here. It seats eight, and is fitted with eight lamps for night riding, and it has a fully stocked bar."

"A bar?" Fargo had never heard of such a thing.

"Mr. Carver's motto is that money is no object," Banner remarked. "He surrounds himself with the very best of everything, from the clothes on his back to the carriages he rides in, to those who work for him."

Which brought up an intriguing point. Fargo glanced at the pair as he went through the gate. "What are you two best at?"

Meachum answered matter-of-factly. "We're his seconds-in-command, you might say. Or, as we prefer, his executive assistants. Each of us previously worked for large corporations back East."

"And it takes the two of you to help Carver run his little business empire?" Fargo said.

"Oh, it's hardly little, sir," Banner responded. "Last year alone, Mr. Carver earned in excess of two million dollars."

Fargo whistled in appreciation. By any standard, two million was a lot of money. Molly hadn't been exaggerating when she'd said Carver was one of the richest men in the territory. He might very well be *the* richest.

One of the coachmen had climbed down to open a door for them. Fargo stepped up and slid across a seat wide enough to sleep on. To say the interior was extravagant was like saying the Rocky Mountains were high. The leather was rich and thick, trimmed in gold, the paneling polished to a sheen. And inset in the back of the seat facing him was the bar, consisting of a mahogany cabinet and shiny counter. "Now I've seen everything."

"This is nothing," Meachum said, entering. "You'll see for yourself soon enough."

Banner followed. "Wait until you see Mr. Carver's riverfront home. It isn't as large as his country estate or the house he owns in the city proper, but it would make a sultan drool with envy."

The coachman closed the door and within moments they were under way.

"How many homes does your boss own?" Fargo casually inquired.

"Seven," Meachum said, then caught himself. "Oh, wait—eight. Last week he purchased property in Atlanta. A plantation, I believe."

Fargo had a lot to ponder as they traveled up one

broad street and down another. Foremost was the question of how someone who basically ran a dry-goods outfit had acquired so much wealth. And where could a man like Carver possibly be going that he needed a frontiersman to guide him? To Denver, maybe? Or even Santa Fe? But if that were the case, Carver could take a stage or ride in his special carriage.

Meachum cleared his throat. "Our employer is looking forward to this meeting, sir. He was extremely pleased when he discovered who you are."

"Why?"

"As we noted, Mr. Carver only hires the best. And you, Mr. Fargo, are widely hailed as the best scout alive. They say there isn't a section of the West you haven't explored."

"I haven't seen all of it yet," Fargo said. He would, though, before he was done. God willing.

Meachum's gaze lowered to Fargo's Colt. "It's also claimed you are marvelously fast and extraordinarily accurate with your firearm. How many men have you killed in your illustrious career, if you don't mind my asking?"

"I do mind," Fargo said coldly. There was nothing illustrious about shooting someone. For him, it was a matter of survival, of kill or be killed. He'd never shot anyone without just cause.

"My apologies, sir," Meachum said. "I didn't mean to offend you."

"It's just that Mr. Carver is also quite adept with a side arm," Banner said, "and he is naturally eager to meet an equal."

The more Fargo learned about Jace Carver, the less he liked. "I hope I don't disappoint him," he said dryly.

"That wouldn't be advisable, sir," Banner said. "Another of Mr. Carver's personal mottos is that disappointments are the trademark of failures and losers. Men of distinction, men like himself, are never disappointed because they won't let themselves be."

"How many mottos does he have?" Fargo managed to ask with a straight face.

"Oh, I can't rightly say, sir," Banner answered. "His private secretary jots down his sayings whenever he comes up with a new one. 'Words of wisdom' is what Mr. Carver calls them. He says that one day he'll write a book and share them with the rest of the world."

Fargo thought it comforting to know that the rich and powerful could be just as idiotic as the poor and meek. "His wife must be awful proud of him," he said, fishing for information.

"Mr. Carver isn't married, sir," Meachum said, running a finger along his waxed mustache. "Nor does he have any inclination to be."

Banner nodded. "Women are playthings to him. They serve one useful purpose and one alone. They're entertaining in bed, but otherwise they're of little consequence."

"Another of his mottos?" Fargo said, barely able to keep the sarcasm out of his voice.

"You're fortunate to receive this invitation," Meachum said. "Scores of people would give anything to be in your shoes. Pardon me, in your boots." He then turned to gaze out the window. "Traffic is light this morning. We should be there in half an hour."

"I can hardly wait," Fargo replied.

4

Jace Carver's version of paradise on earth was located on a lush fifty-acre plot bordering the Kansas River. A gravel drive linked a gold-gilt gate to a stately, imposing yellow house situated amid towering oaks and maples. Beds of flowers, clipped hedges, and trimmed grass testified to how meticulously the grounds were maintained by workers, who, like the coach drivers, wore yellow work clothes.

There was a huge stable, a corral filled with horses, a woodshed, and various outbuildings, all looking as if they had been built the day before, and all painted a vivid yellow. A man chopping wood, another loading hay onto a wagon, and a third by the corral all wore garments of the same hue.

A long dock and an adjoining building, likewise yellow, bordered the waterway. Berthed at the dock was a canary yellow sternwheel riverboat, the crewmen moving about on her decked out as brightly as everything else.

Armed guards were stationed at the gate. Fargo observed others patrolling the property and noticed that unlike the rest of Carver's hirelings, the guards wore normal attire so they wouldn't be walking targets. Jace Carver might be eccentric, but he wasn't stupid.

"That's Mr. Carver's private riverboat," Meachum mentioned. "The *Yellow Rose,* he calls her."

"I wonder why," Fargo said, and had to ask the question that had been nagging at him ever since he saw the pair of coachmen. "Why all the yellow?"

"I should think the reason would be obvious, sir,"

Banner said. "Mr. Carver gets what he wants. Mr. Carver wants the sun. When that proved to be a trophy beyond even his grasp, our current attire proved to be an acceptable substitute."

Fargo was tempted to tell them to turn the carriage around and take him back to Molly's, not wanting to meet this egomaniac. But he had come this far. And, truth to tell, he still was curious to see what Jace Carver was like in person.

The carriage rolled to a stop at the base of broad marble steps. A middle-aged man in a yellow butler's uniform descended, bearing a silver tray containing a pitcher of water and three crystal glasses. He gave a courtly bow as Meachum and Banner emerged.

"Our lord and master conveys his warm greetings, gentlemen. He requests that you bring his guest around back."

"Will do, Smithers," Meachum said.

Fargo stepped down and arched his spine to relieve a kink. He spied a maid cleaning an upstairs window, not the least bit surprised that her uniform was—what else?—yellow. He supposed he should look at the bright side. At least Carver wasn't fond of pink.

"Would you care for some liquid refreshment, sir?" Smithers asked, holding out the tray.

"Liquid refreshment?" Fargo repeated out of amusement.

"Water, sir?"

"What, no whiskey?" Fargo started up the steps but Banner called his name and motioned to the left.

"This way, if you please."

"After you," Fargo said. Banner walked off. Meachum, however, didn't move, so Fargo clarified his request by stating, "After both of you."

The butler fell into step beside him. "I apologize for not having whiskey, sir. No one advised me to do so. If you'll be so kind as to specify which brand you prefer, I'll bring a glass to you on the veranda."

"At this time of the morning?"

Smithers's forehead creased. "Oh. I see, sir. You

were jesting. Very droll of you, sir. Worthy of the master himself."

Fargo studied him. Smithers seemed sane enough, but any man who would consent to wearing yellow clothes all the time might just be a few nuts shy of a bushel. Bending so that Meachum and Banner wouldn't overhear, Fargo said, "Tell me something. Just between the two of us, why do you let Carver dress you in that getup and go around calling him your 'lord and master'?"

The butler coughed, started to grin, then composed himself and whispered, "Just between us, sir? Then let me say that for enough money, I would perform my duties in a dress and call my employer the Almighty."

Fargo stifled a laugh. "Is that the way it is with most of his staff?"

"I daresay, sir, with all of them," Smithers said. "Quite frankly, the general consensus is that Mr. Carver is a cross between a clown and Attila the Hun."

"I'm beginning to understand. What about those two?" Fargo inquired, nodding at the self-styled executive assistants.

"Again, sir, it is commonly held that both Mr. Meachum and Mr. Banner would benefit greatly from surgery."

"I don't follow."

"To remove the broomsticks stuck up there asses, sir."

Fargo couldn't contain his laughter if he tried. Meachum and Banner glanced back, so Fargo pointed at the yellow woodshed and said, "Does your boss have someone paint the wood yellow, too?"

Plainly, neither thought it the least bit funny.

"A word to wise, sir," Meachum said sternly. "Mr. Carver takes a dim view of those who criticize him or his idiosyncrasies. Those who do so don't last long in his employ."

"Then it's a good thing I'm not working for him,"

Fargo countered. And based on all that he had learned, the likelihood that he ever would was slim to none.

Meachum and Banner walked around the corner of the house.

"Sir?" Smithers quickly whispered to Fargo. "I trust you won't forget my reference to Attila the Hun? Jace Carver isn't someone you want to trifle with. He's a dangerous man. Extremely dangerous," the butler stressed.

Fargo was going to ask what Smithers meant but the two high-and-mighty assistants had stopped to wait for them to catch up and from that point on they couldn't talk in private.

Giant maples overspread the footpath, while on their left, fragrant flowers filled a plot being tended to by a gardener in yellow overalls.

Feminine laughter perked Fargo's ears as they came to the rear. Seated at a yellow table, in yellow chairs, were three young beauties in skimpy yellow dresses. One was a redhead, one a blonde, one a brunette. Huddled together, they twittered merrily.

"Quite over there, you damned hussies!" someone harshly demanded. "Can't you see I'm trying to concentrate?"

As if a switch had been thrown, the trio sobered and straightened, the redhead calling out, "We're awfully sorry, Mr. Carver."

Fargo didn't know what he was expecting. Maybe a loon in an expensive yellow suit. Maybe an immaculate gentleman attired in the height of fashion. But Jace Carver was as ordinary as ordinary could be. About five-feet-eleven, stocky in the chest but slim at the waist, he had an angular face crowned by curly black hair. His most notable feature were his striking green eyes, blazing with an uncommon inner vitality. Carver wore a brown shirt, and black pants and shoes. Not a lick of yellow anywhere.

After all Fargo had heard, it was a bit of a letdown.

Then he saw what Carver was doing and his interest was rekindled.

Standing beside a small white ball balanced on a thin piece of wood, the lord of the manor was swinging an odd sort of stick back and forth, practicing, evidently. It took a few moments for Fargo to realize what they were; a golf club, a golf ball, and a tee. Fargo had heard about the game but he couldn't recall ever seeing it played. Suddenly he realized Carver's green eyes were fixed on him.

"Ah, Mr. Fargo! I'll be with you momentarily. I'm about to tee off." Carver adopted a stooped-over stance and held the club close to the ball. Pausing, he looked up. "Do you play, by any chance?"

"Can't say as I ever have," Fargo answered. The game was for blue bloods, for those who could afford to while away their hours smacking a little ball all over creation. In that regard it was a lot like tennis and racquetball. Few west of the Mississippi had ever *heard* of the game, let alone played it.

"A pity," Jace Carver said. "Golf is the sport of kings. It has done more to civilize our society than all the laws ever passed."

Fargo didn't quite see how the two were related, nor did he really care. "Was I invited to breakfast or to watch you play?"

"Bear with me a moment," Carver said. He gazed off toward a tiny pennant fluttering at the end of a thin pole, then focused on the golf ball to the exclusion of all else. Everyone was deathly quiet, supremely still, as if it were taboo to talk or even move. After another few seconds, the club whipped in a tight arc. The ball sailed in a long, sloping curve, coming to earth within a few yards of the pole.

Applause broke out, the women squealing and laughing while Meachum declared, "Well done, sir!"

"Almost a hole in one!" Banner said.

Smithers, not to be left out, called out, "Magnificent shot, sir!"

Jace Carver was tremendously pleased with himself.

44

Handing the club to a young man who was holding a long leather bag full of other clubs, he hooked his thumbs in his belt and sauntered to the veranda. "I tell you, Mr. Fargo," he said, "if I could, I'd retire and spend the rest of my days doing nothing but playing golf."

"What's stopping you?" Fargo made a gesture that encompassed the grand house and the lavishly landscaped grounds. "It's not as if you don't have enough money to live on."

"My good fellow, you've uttered the blasphemy of blasphemies," Carver said, smiling. "There's no such thing as 'enough.' The more I acquire, the more I want to acquire. The more I *must* acquire."

"You make it sound as if you have no choice."

"In a sense, I don't," Carver responded. "Adding to my wealth is a necessity, a deeply personal need I doubt you are capable of comprehending."

Fargo resented the insult. "Do you make it a habit to look down your nose at others?"

Carver halted at an empty table next to the ladies. "Please don't misconstrue. It's merely that most people find it difficult to understand." He beckoned. "You're not the only one to suggest I call it quits. Even Smithers there has said I should take more time to smell the roses. But as much as I might want to, I can't. Something deep inside compels me to constantly reach out for more, more, more."

"So you won't stop until you're the richest man alive?" Fargo said, joining Carver. He didn't like the way Meachum and Banner seemed to always flank him, as if he weren't trustworthy enough to be permitted close to their employer.

"The richest in the country," Jace Carver said in all seriousness. "After that goal is met, who knows? I like to think of the world as a succulent oyster, and I do so love seafood." He pointed at the chair he wanted Fargo to use. "Please. Have a seat and we'll eat."

Fargo reached out to pull the chair back, but before he could Smithers was there, doing it for him.

"Allow me, sir."

Carver waited for the manservant to do the same for him, then said, "Instruct the kitchen staff to begin serving. And warn Louis that if my milk isn't the right temperature this time, he can pack his bags and take the next ship back home."

As Smithers hurried into the house, Fargo leaned back. "The right temperature?"

"I like to have a glass of warm milk with my breakfast. A habit of mine, instilled when I was a lad. My new cook came highly recommended as one of the best chefs in Paris. And while he does make delicious *profiteroles,* he's a bumbling incompetent at heating a simple glass of milk. Several times I've shown him how warm I like it, but he just can't get it right. Either it's too cool or too hot."

"Why not heat it yourself?" Fargo said.

"Spoken like someone who has no concept of the true value of money. Look around you. Wealth is power. Wealth is luxury. Wealth is never doing for yourself what others can do for you." Carver shifted toward his lieutenants. "Where's Timmons? He should add those to my words of wisdom."

"We don't know where he is, Mr. Carver," Meachum said.

"We just got back from the city, sir, remember?" Banner chimed in.

The redhead at the next table piped up reminding Carver, "You sent Timmons upstairs a while ago for some papers."

"Oh. So I did." Carver frowned. "I should keep a tablet handy. It's tragic to waste any of my verbal pearls."

Fargo couldn't get over how everyone bowed and scraped around his host, how they treated him as if he were a crowned head of Europe and they were his lowly subjects. "I've heard about the book you plan to write," Fargo said.

"One day," Carver said. "It'll contain all the wisdom I've gleaned over the years, all the knowledge I've acquired. Everyone will want a copy. It will be a staple in every home, right beside their Bible."

Damned if the man wasn't serious, Fargo observed. "Let's get down to business. Why do you need a scout?"

"First things first," Carver, said, gesturing. "I trust you're hungry? After we eat we'll discuss my proposition."

A procession of yellow-clad staff filed out of the house, men and women alike, bearing tray after tray. The first contained a heaping mountain of scrambled eggs, another bacon, another sausage, another toast and jam, and on and on it went. There was fresh fruit, bananas, berries, and nuts, enough food to feed half of Kansas City. One by one the hired help filed past the lord of the manor, and Carver only had to point to have food ladled onto his plate.

Fargo wanted some eggs and reached for the tray but the woman holding it shifted so he couldn't take it from her. Instead, she spooned some onto his plate.

Jace Carver chuckled. "My people are well trained. They know I insist on abiding by the amenities, even when my guests do not."

Again Fargo had been subtly slighted, and it rankled him. When the next staff member stepped to his side, Fargo grabbed hold of the edge of the silver serving tray and wrestled it loose. Several strips spilled but he didn't care. Setting it down, he selected the pieces that *he* wanted.

All movement ceased. All eyes were on Carver, who stiffened and glowered. His lips compressed into a thin line and he appeared poised to leap out of his chair in a rage. But with a visible effort, he regained control of his surging emotions and said, "If you'll pardon my bluntness, that was terribly crass. I pay these people good wages to perform good work. Kindly permit them to earn it."

"I don't like being waited on hand and foot," Fargo declared. "I'm a grown man. I can fend for myself."

Now it was Carver who had been slighted and he reddened. "Your attitude, my good man, leaves a lot to be desired."

"Listen to the kettle call the pot black."

Someone—one of the women, perhaps—gasped. Tension crackled like lightning. Smithers looked as if he had just swallowed a walnut, shell and all. Meachum and Banner grew as flinty as quartz, and each started to slide a hand under their jackets.

Carver's eyes were molten pits of wrath. Yet, inexplicably, he didn't vent his notorious temper. He didn't rant or curse or threaten. He merely forked a piece of sausage into his mouth and chewed a bit, then said, "We're getting off on the wrong foot, and I do so want us to get along."

Fargo wasn't the only one who was surprised. The faces of many of the others were open books, showing surprise at their master's benevolence.

Smithers, in an attempt to pacify his employer, remarked, "I suppose, sir, that the customs of polite society don't matter a great deal to someone who spends a good deal of his time living in the wilderness."

Carver stopped chewing. "I hadn't thought of that. An excellent point. To a man like Mr. Fargo, here, all this must be the height of pretension."

"It's damned silly," Fargo agreed.

Again someone gasped. But Jace Carver was either less of a monster than he was rumored to be, or he was a lot shrewder than most gave him credit for. Because all he did was laugh heartily. Everyone else promptly followed his example, their mirth as hollow as the ringing of a cracked bell.

"Touché, Mr. Fargo," Carver said. "So why don't I forgo the 'silliness,' as you call it, and cut right to the chase. Would that satisfy you?"

Fargo was spooning scrambled eggs into his mouth and contented himself with a grunt. He was tired of

Carver, tired of all the nonsense. As soon as he finished, he intended to leave.

"I'll take that as a 'yes,'" his host said. Placing his fork down, Carver made a pensive tepee of his fingers. "As you've been informed, I am in need of a skilled scout. Of someone as versed in life on the plains as I am in business matters."

"I've crossed the plains once or twice," Fargo mentioned.

"You're much too humble. A hundred times would be more accurate." Carver paused. "When my pathetic excuse for a cousin, Harold Pinder, told me he had met you, I took it as an omen. I contacted several friends who keep up on such things, and they all agreed that without exception, you're the best there is at what you do."

"Jim Bridger and Kit Carson are just as good."

"Perhaps. But Bridger is well past his prime. And Carson is off who-knows-where." Carver speared his fork into a strip of bacon, cut it into thirds with his knife, then slid a morsel into his mouth.

Fargo deliberately picked up the greasiest piece on his plate with his fingers and stuffed the whole thing in. Chomping lustily, he smacked his lips, acting as if he didn't have any table manners whatsoever.

Carver frowned but said nothing. "Word has it you've even lived among the Indians on occasion. That you know their heathen ways better than anyone."

Fargo continued eating. The sooner he was done, the sooner he could get out of there, and the sooner he could crawl under the covers with Molly. The thought of her, and of their lovemaking the night before, brought a smile to his lips.

"Does this apply to the Pawnees, too?" Carver asked.

"I've had some dealings with them," Fargo said. Most frontiersmen had. By and large, the Pawnees were peaceable enough. The tribe had never taken the warpath against the white man, although now and then small bands of renegades made trouble for a few out-lying settlements.

"Then you're aware of how conniving they can be," Carver said. "How deceitful. How treacherous."

"A few, maybe."

Jace Carver set down his knife and fork. "Be realistic. My dealings with them have taught me they're opportunists who would just as soon stab a person in the back as look at them. Some of the red devils have been causing trouble for me, and all because I refuse to give in to their unseemly demands."

Fargo plucked another bacon strip from his plate and crunched into it. "Mind explaining?" he asked with his mouth full.

Just then a small man in a baggy suit emerged and hustled to their table, bearing a document of some sort in one hand and a leather case in the other. He had an oval chin, a bald pate, and a huge Adam's apple, lending him the aspect of a turkey buzzard.

"Ah Timmons. About time," Carver said severely. "Mr. Fargo, this is my private secretary. I sent him to obtain something you will want to see."

"Which is?"

Carver snatched the document from his underling, who cringed as if in fear of being struck. "Before I show you, there's something I must explain. I trust you've heard about the small settlements springing up along the Platte River?"

Fargo admitted he had. There were only a few, made up of hardy souls trying to eke out a living as farmers. Some were pilgrims who had headed for the Oregon Country or California and decided the fertile lowland along the Platte was good enough to suit them. In his estimation, though, the sodbusters were asking for trouble. They were all alone in the middle of the vast prairie, in country freely roamed by the Pawnees, the Sioux, and the Arapaho. And the Indians had made no secret of the fact they didn't like intruders.

"Four settlements, at last count," Carver had gone

on. "Remote, isolated, at the mercy of the elements, surrounded by hostiles everywhere. It's a brutal existence. Without a reliable source of supplies, they won't last."

About to treat himself to a slice of toast layered thick with jam, Fargo looked up. He had an inkling of where the talk was leading. "Let me guess. You're their supplier?"

"Them, and most everyone else along the frontier." Carver leaned forward on his elbows. "When I was fifteen, I learned the most important lesson of my life. A friend told me that he wanted to buy a folding knife with antler grips for his father's birthday, but he couldn't find one anywhere. I had another friend, though, who owned one. So I went to my second friend and talked him into selling it to me for five dollars. Then I turned around and sold it to my first friend for ten. On that one little transaction, I made five dollars profit."

"So?"

"So it taught me that people are willing to pay through the nose for things they want. It taught me that the road to riches lies in being the supplier of those wants. As the middleman, the wholesaler, I can mark up prices to whatever the market will bear."

Fargo surveyed the house, the stable, the grounds. "I'd say you learned the lesson well."

Jace Carver laughed. "That I did! I scrimped, I saved, I made the right contacts. At first I supplied only a few goods to a handful of general stores. As time went on, I added to my client list. Now all the major outlets in the city are under my control. I also supply every general store in every settlement along the Kansas and Missouri rivers. And I have an exclusive contract with the army. In short, I'm the most powerful man around."

As much as Fargo might wish it were otherwise, there was no denying the truth. "There's a point to all this?"

Carver thrust the document across the table. "This

is my contract with the general store at Finlay's Bend, the furthermost settlement on the Platte River. Per the terms, I've agreed to take supplies to them twice a year in exchange for a specified sum."

Fargo hardly gave it a glance. "You still haven't told me why you need my services."

"Because I've run into a problem. The last two times I sent men out, they were stopped by a band of Pawnees who demanded tribute to cross their territory. An outrageous tribute. When my men objected, the Pawnees forced them at gunpoint to hand over their valuable goods." Carver's voice became a gravely growl. "That *won't* happen again. This time I'm going along to personally insure all the merchandise gets through."

"Since you already know where Finlay's Bend is, what use would I be?" Fargo asked, genuinely puzzled.

"If possible, I'd rather avoid a clash with the heathens. I need you to help me avoid them by guiding the wagons over a different route than the one they would normally take." Carver held up a hand before Fargo had a chance to speak. "Before you decline, keep two things in mind. First, by avoiding the Pawnees, we avoid bloodshed. Second, and most importantly, without the supplies I'm bringing, the homesteaders at Finlay's Bend won't make it through the upcoming winter. Many will give up and return to the States, failures. Some will starve. By helping me, you're helping them, helping to save lives, save whole families. Surely that's worthwhile enough to merit your help?"

Fargo lost his appetite. The only thing worse than being caught in a box canyon by a bunch of marauding warriors, he mused, was being boxed into a bad situation by his own conscience.

"So what do you say, Trailsman?" Jace Carver asked.

Skye Fargo stared at the other man for a moment, knowing that he had but one possible response. "When do we leave?"

5

The next morning the *Yellow Rose* lifted anchor, eased from the dock, and churned northward up the Missouri River. Skye Fargo brought the Ovaro on board right before they left and placed it in a holding pen along with a dozen other fine mounts from Carver's stable. They'd need every one.

Jace Carver had insisted on bringing Meachum and Banner, saying that they were indispensable. So was Timmons, who was none too happy about being made to go. Carver also instructed Smithers to pack a bag and join their "little expedition." In addition, eight of Carver's personal guards, each armed with twin Remington revolvers, a new Spencer, and a Bowie, were included in the party.

Fargo tried to convince Carver to leave Timmons and Smithers behind. Neither was essential. In a fight with the Pawnees, they would be next to useless. And Fargo had taken a liking to the butler and didn't care to see him harmed.

But Carver wouldn't listen. "You mind your business and I'll mind mine," was how he put it. "I need my secretary to take important notes and record my words of wisdom for posterity. As for Smithers, surely you don't expect me to wait on myself? As it is I'll be roughing it. I should have brought half a dozen of my personal staff."

Fargo could see that arguing would be useless, so he let the matter drop.

Another disagreement developed, though, the first afternoon out. They were lounging on the hurricane deck on the upper level when Jace Carver glanced at his guards and remarked, "I almost hope the damn Pawnees do give us trouble. My men have enough artillery to blast the entire tribe to ribbons."

"No one is to shoot unless I give the order," Fargo said. He had taken Carver at his word about wanting to avoid bloodshed and wasn't going to stand for senseless slaughter.

"Did I just hear correctly? Since when do you give orders? In case I didn't make it sufficiently clear, I'm in complete and total command. I, and I alone, give commands."

"Not once we're out on the prairie," Fargo said.

Carver bristled like an angry porcupine. "Don't overstep yourself. I've already tolerated more abuse from you than I ever have from anyone else, all for the sake of safely getting my merchandise through. But I draw the line at insubordination. I lead, you follow. It's as simple as that."

Fargo's patience was wearing thin. "Then lead your wagons to Finlay's Bend yourself. Once we disembark, I'm going my own way. You can have your money back." Carver had agreed to pay him the princely sum of one thousand dollars, half in advance, but no amount of money was worth the aggravation he had to endure.

"You're bluffing."

Fargo didn't say anything.

"If you drop out, we might not make it. All those poor homesteaders will be left stranded. You won't allow that," Carver said confidently.

As much as Fargo wanted to help the settlers, the issue was too important for him to back down. Jace Carver gloried in riding roughshod over people. Unless they established then and there that he, and not Carver, had the final say-so out on the plains, there was no predicting how much trouble Carver would get them into.

"Damn your bones!" the millionaire declared when Fargo still didn't respond. Rising from his deck chair, he said crisply, "Who do you think you are? You'll answer me or I'll have you keelhauled. Remember, the captain and every crewman on the *Yellow Rose* are in my personal employ."

Smithers, who had been standing beside Carver's chair, awaiting his boss's next whim, tried to intervene. "Perhaps a compromise could be worked out, sir—" He got no further.

With the speed of a striking serpent, Jace Carver wheeled and gripped the butler by the front of his shirt. "How dare you? Why do you keep defending him? Have you forgotten who pays your salary?"

Fargo had had enough. Slowly rising, he took a single step to the right so he could keep an eye on Meachum and Banner and the guards lining the port rail. "Take your hands off him," he said quietly.

Carver's features were contorted in bestial ferocity. His true self was showing, proving all the rumors true. "What did you just say?"

"Take your hands off Smithers."

"Or what?" Carver laughed, an icy, brittle burst laced with contempt. "You're one man against thirty. My boys will cut you down where you stand."

"I'd get off a shot or two," Fargo said. "At you."

Carver's free hand was clenching and unclenching as if he yearned to clamp it around Fargo's throat. "The last time someone had the nerve to buck me, I had him tied to a tree and whipped. Don't make the same mistake. If I want to manhandle my butler, I will. If I want to wipe out the Pawnees, I will. No one defies me. *Ever.*"

Fargo's right hand flashed so swiftly that the Colt was out and cocked and the muzzle pressed against Carver's forehead before anyone else could so much as blink. "For the last time, let go of him or buck out in gore."

The guards galvanized to life and started to bring their Spencers to bear, but they froze at a sharp word from Meachum. Banner partially drew a revolver from under his jacket, then stopped. Meek little Timmons was gawking like a schoolboy witnessing a schoolyard dispute, too scared to do anything.

None of the riverboat's crew were present, but somewhere someone was bawling that there was trouble on the hurricane deck, and that the captain was needed.

Jace Carver's tongue flicked across his lips. He stared into Fargo's eyes, his own undergoing a change. "You'd do it, wouldn't you? You'd kill me over a trifle?"

Fargo waited. He had said all he was going to. The outcome was now entirely in Carver's hands.

"You have grit, Trailsman, but you're a fool. You risk throwing your life away for someone you hardly know. Why?"

The guards stood stock-still, but Fargo noted that Banner was edging to the left for a clear shot. Meachum had his hand under his jacket and was slinking to the right.

Carver gestured, and both men halted. "No one is to lift a finger, you hear me! This is between Mr. Fargo and myself." Peeling his fingers from the butler's shirt, Carver smoothed it. "You're a fine manservant, but you're not worth dying over." He patted Smithers on the head as someone might pat a favorite pet. "No hard feelings, I trust? You know how I can get."

"No hard feelings, sir," Smithers demurely said.

Fargo stepped back and twirled the Colt into its holster with a flourish. Delving into a pocket, he produced the wad of bills Carver had given him. "Either I'm in charge once we head out across the prairie or you can have your money back here and now."

The most powerful man in Kansas City made no attempt to take it. Raising his voice, he said so that all could hear, "Take a good look, gentlemen. What we have here is a rare individual. A man of principle, of conviction. A man who lives by his own rules and doesn't back down to anyone. A man very much like myself."

Fargo heard footsteps and saw the captain and several roustabouts rush up.

Carver motioned them to a standstill. "All is well, Captain Trent. I'm in no peril. Go on about your duties."

Grumbling, the men in yellow complied.

"Now then," Carver said to Fargo, "where does that leave you and me?" Nonchalantly sinking into his deck chair, he placed his hands behind his head. "At a snap of my fingers I could yet have you slain. But after seeing you draw, I have no doubt you'd gun me down before my men got off a shot. Hardly a viable option is it?" He paused. "By the same token, I can't let you prevail. I have my own principles to think of. So perhaps Smithers had the right idea, after all. Perhaps a compromise is in order."

"I'm listening," Fargo said.

"You may have overall charge once we leave Fort Kearney. I will order my men to do as you tell them or suffer the consequences. They're not to open fire on the Pawnees unless you give the word." Carver's eyes narrowed in spiteful menace. "But make no mistake. I reserve the right to override any decision you make that's contrary to my best interests. Just as I would with anyone else in my organization. Do we have a deal?"

The proposal sounded fair enough, but Fargo knew better. In effect, what Carver was saying was that when all was said and done, he would do as he damn well pleased. A small concession had been made, nothing more. Still, it was the best Fargo could hope for. Shoving the bills back into his pocket, he said, "We have a deal."

"Then let's forgive and forget, shall we?" Carver said. "Have a seat. Smithers, drinks for the both of us to toast our new understanding."

Fargo stayed on his feet. "What's this about Fort Kearney?" He had been under the impression that the wagons would be waiting for them at the confluence of the Missouri River and the Platte, and from there they would make a beeline for Finlay's Bend.

"Didn't I tell you?" Carver said. "Four fully loaded wagons and another ten men are waiting for us at the post. They left Kansas City weeks ago. I planned all along to catch up once I found a competent scout."

Some things just weren't adding up. "Four wagon-loads for just one settlement?" Fargo said. "It should be enough to last them years."

"Oh, no. You have it all wrong. We're stopping at all four new settlements, unloading a wagon at each," Carver elaborated. "Finlay's Bend is our last stop, not the only one."

"You never said anything about this before."

Jace Carver shrugged. "Does it matter? We have to pass each of the settlements on our way to Finlay's Bend anyway."

On the face of it, it made sense. Since Carver supplied goods to all four communities, delivering the merchandise in one trip was sound business practice. But Fargo resented being kept in the dark. And he couldn't shake the nagging feeling that something else wasn't quite right.

For instance, why was it a man like Jace Carver, a man devoted only to himself and to money, was so worried about the welfare of a small group of home-steaders off in the middle of nowhere? How was it that someone who treated every other human being as if they were of less account than the dirt under his feet was so willing to personally lead a hazardous undertaking to aid people he didn't know?

The butler returned with a glass of whiskey for Fargo and a glass of Scotch for Carver, who raised his drink in salute.

"To a speedy, safe journey."

Everyone looked at Fargo, expecting him to do the decent thing and offer a toast of his own. "To no blood being spilled," he said, then inhaled his drink in three gulps and gave the glass back to the butler. "I'm going to check on my horse," he announced, walking off. Not that the Ovaro needed checking. He just wanted to be alone with his thoughts for a while.

"There's plenty of oats if it needs some," Jace Carver mentioned. "I keep enough on board to feed every animal in the Fifth Cavalry."

Descending the companionway, Fargo made for the special holding pen on the main deck between the boiler room and the engine room. The horses were cramped for space but sheltered from the hot sun and the wind. The stallion had a corner to itself and was standing with its head hung low.

"You don't like this setup very much, do you?" Fargo asked as he reached over the top rail to stroke behind the pinto's ears. "I can't say as I blame you. I've stepped in it up to my knees, I reckon."

In his saddlebags, stored in the tack room, were a brush and currycomb. Fetching them, Fargo opened the gate and entered the pen. Due to the constant noise and clatter of the vessel, the horses were skittish. Most pranced and nickered as he threaded among them to the far corner. He had just begun brushing the pinto when a yellow uniform materialized out of the shadows.

"I'm supposed to be getting some cheese from the pantry for Mr. High-and-Mighty," Smithers said. "But I needed to thank you."

"One of these days he'll fly off the handle like that and no one will be around to help you," Fargo noted.

"I know, I know." The butler sighed. "I've reached the conclusion that no amount of money is worth the aggravation I put up with. Maybe after we get back, I'll tender my resignation and seek a job elsewhere."

"Maybe?" Fargo said.

"It's not easy to do, friend," Smithers said. "I make three times as much working for him as I would any-where else." He scanned the immediate vicinity, then said softly, "One good turn deserves another. I came to warn you. After you left, Mr. Carver and Meachum were talking. I didn't catch it all, but I heard enough to gather that Mr. Carver resents how you stood up to him, and he's plotting to do you harm."

"When?"

"I don't know, I'm afraid. But I would be on my guard, were I you. My employer won't rest until he has paid you back.

Fargo stepped to the rails. "You're risking your job telling me this."

Smithers smiled. "Don't fret on my account, sir. If anyone mentions seeing us together to Mr. Carver, I'll simply say I stopped to ask whether you wanted some cheese."

"He'll believe you?"

"Why shouldn't he? I am, if nothing else, highly efficient." Smithers began to back away. "Please, sir. Take utmost care. I rather like you, and I would hate for you to end up as so many of Mr. Carver's other enemies have."

"How do you mean?" Fargo asked, but the butler was already hurrying off.

Had Carver killed before? was the question Fargo spent the next half hour mulling over. It would seem unlikely, with all Carver stood to lose if he were caught. Then again, Carver's terrible temper, combined with his tyrannical nature, were a fiery mix. All it would take would be the right spark to set him off.

Toward evening, Fargo ventured back up onto the upper deck. Boisterous voices drew him to the main cabin where supper was just about to be served. Three long tables had been set with crystal glasses and fine china. Bottles of wine were lined up in rows. Overhead, as radiant as the sun, hung a pair of glittering chandeliers.

Jace Carver was at the head table, along with Meachum and Banner, Timmons, and the silver-haired Captain Trent. Across from them, much to Fargo's surprise, sat the three lovelies he had last seen on the veranda at the riverfront estate—the redhead, the blonde, and the brunette. He'd had no idea they were on the *Yellow Rose*.

"Mr. Fargo!" Carver cheerfully exclaimed, in fine fettle. A half-empty bottle of wine at his elbow was the likely reason. "I was about to send Smithers to find you. It's customary for everyone to attend the evening meal."

Not quite everyone, Fargo noticed. At the second table sat the eight armed guards, their Spencers propped against the wall. But only a few of the ship's crew—the mate, the engineer, and two burly roustabouts—were present, at the last table.

"I've saved a seat for you," Carver said, nodding at an empty seat across from him, on the same side as the women.

Fargo walked around and sank down in the upholstered chair.

The redhead was next to him, and she smiled at him warmly. "Pleased to make your acquaintance, mister. I'm Paula. This here is Dulcie"—she jerked her thumb at the blonde—"and the other lady is Tricia."

"Lady?" Jace Carver had overheard her. "You flatter yourselves. The truth of the matter, Mr. Fargo, is that I met the three of them at Lucky Alice's house of ill repute and invited them to stay with me until I tire of their company."

Paula pursed her full red lips. "Anyone ever tell you that you're a real charmer, Mr. Carver? If so, they lied through their teeth."

As unpredictable as ever, Carver chuckled instead of taking offense. "She's a feisty wench, isn't she?" He snickered. "I like a girl with sauce in her veins. They make much better lovers, don't you think?"

Captain Trent seemed embarrassed for the ladies. Meachum and Banner, on the other hand, were openly leering at them, while Timmons had blushed at the mention of lovemaking and was pretending to be interested in his silverware.

"Oh, I don't know," Fargo responded. "Any woman is a good lover if the man she's making love to is any good."

Paula, Dulcie, and Tricia laughed and clapped. Paula said, "Spoken like a man who has more than a little experience under his belt." She winked at Fargo mischievously.

Carver's good mood seemed to fade. Pouring himself another glass of wine, he upended it, then smacked the glass onto the table. "It seems, Mr. Fargo, that no matter how hard I try to be civil, you insist on getting my goat every chance you get." He waged a finger at the females. "Thank God I brought these vixens along to entertain me and keep me warm on those chilly nights out on the prairie."

"What?"

"Is your hearing gone, as well as your sense of humor?" Carver rejoined. "They're going with us to Finlay's Bend."

"For their sakes, please reconsider," Fargo said. "It's too risky."

"Life is a risk. And I'm paying these trollops extremely well. They have no cause to complain."

Fargo found Carver's arrogance appalling. "They will if the Pawnees get their hands on them."

"We'll have close to two-dozen armed men in our party. The women will be well protected."

"How many of your men are Indian fighters?" Fargo asked. "How many have eyes in the backs of their heads and can sleep with one eye open?"

Carver stifled a yawn. "What's your point?"

"The women just aren't safe. Renegade Pawnees or Sioux can sneak into camp whenever they want."

"Spare me. You make the heathens sound almost supernatural. But they're not. They're flesh and blood, just like you and me. And they can be caught and killed, just like a white man."

Fargo realized he could talk himself hoarse and it wouldn't do any good. But he had to try, if only for the sake of the doves. "Earlier you agreed to let me handle things out on the prairie. And I don't want them along."

Some of the others glanced at Carver as if anticipating an explosion, but he merely sneered. "We're not out on the prairie yet, are we? And earlier I also reminded you that I have the final say. The tarts are going whether you agree or not."

Fargo was in a bind. He could still back out of their arrangement, still tell Carver to go jump off the bow and go his own way when the *Yellow Rose* reached the Platte River. But that wouldn't help the women. Carver would still head west, still take them along, still expose them to deadly danger, or worse. It left Fargo no choice but to go along and do what he could to protect them. "I'm sorry," he said to Paula. "I tried."

"And it was very sweet of you," the redhead said, touching his cheek. "But really, you're worried over nothing. Mr. Carver won't let any harm come to us. He hates to sleep alone."

Both the doves and Jace Carver chortled at her joke, but to Fargo it wasn't the least bit funny. They had no idea of what they were letting themselves in for. Seeing Smithers approach, he asked, "Have any more of that whiskey on board?"

"The best money can buy," the butler confirmed.

"I need some. And leave the bottle."

"That's the spirit!" Carver enthused. "Eat, drink, and be merry! Think of our enterprise as a glorious adventure!"

It was more like rank stupidity, Fargo thought. When Smithers brought the liquor, he rolled some on his tongue, then swallowed, savoring the smooth warmth that spread down through his chest and stomach.

"On to more pleasant matters," Carver said. "Smithers, where's our food? I'm half starved!"

"We're about to start serving, sir."

Fargo had been on riverboats before. The fare was generally simple, and supplemented by whatever game could be bagged on shore nearby. He should have known that wouldn't be good enough for Jace Carver.

A procession of hired help clad in yellow filed in.

Some Fargo recognized as being part of the kitchen staff at the riverfront property. They brought appetizers fit for a royal palace; snapper soup, chicken soup, mushrooms soaked in butter, fresh baked dinner rolls, and more. The guards and crewmen wolfed it down as if they hadn't eaten in a month. And why not? Rarely, if ever, were they treated to so sumptuous a feast.

Next came the main course. Or, rather, main *courses*. Roast duck. Roast venison. A slab of beef. A platter of fish garnished with lemon and parsley. Loaves of bread barely out of the oven. Vegetables galore. Even corn on the cob.

Fargo ate sparingly. The others paid him no mind except for Paula, who leaned closer at one point midway through the meal.

"Don't let Mr. Carver get to you. He's not worth losing sleep over."

"I was thinking of you, not him," Fargo said, and received a gentle squeeze on his arm.

"We're grateful. We honestly are. But we're all big girls. We're going into this with our eyes open." Paula grinned. "And Carver wasn't kidding. We are being paid really well. More for a month with him than we'd earn in an entire year anywhere else."

"So that makes it right?" Fargo said, refilling his glass. All these people willing to swallow their dignity for money was starting to depress him.

"No, I suppose it doesn't," Paula confessed. "But this is a once-in-a-lifetime opportunity. A chance for us to get ahead. How can we say no?"

"I just hope you don't live to regret it."

Jace Carver had been talking with Captain Trent, but now he turned toward them and said much more loudly than was called for, "Look at you two! Rather cozy, talking so that no one else can hear. What about?"

Fargo had rarely wanted to punch anyone as much as he did the smirking bastard across the table. "None of your damn business."

"Fair enough," Carver said amiably. "But tell me something else. They say that you're quite the ladies' man. Since you've lived with Indians, I can't help wonder if perhaps you've shared your bed with a few squaws."

"My personal life is my own affair," Fargo snapped.

"Don't get all huffy on me," Carver said, laughing. "I only wanted to know what it's like. I've never slept with a squaw. Is it true they have lice in their hair? And that they stink to high heaven because they don't bathe regularly?"

In the act of raising his glass, Fargo slammed it down, spilling some of the whiskey, then he rose. "I'm turning in," he announced and stalked out into the night before he did something Jace Carver would regret. Behind him, the room erupted in laughter.

Pausing, Fargo breathed deep of the brisk, dank air before making his way toward his compartment, situated toward the bow. Most of the boat was well lit by lamps, but not the passageway he had to take. He didn't think much of it until he was almost to his door.

Suddenly, four shapes loomed out of the darkness and a gruff voice growled, "We've been waitin' for you, mate. We don't much like how you've been givin' the boss a hard time. So we aim to teach you some manners."

6

Skye Fargo hadn't fallen out of the sky with the last rain. He knew who had put the four crewmen up to waylaying him. No one did anything on the *Yellow Rose* without Jace Carver's say-so.

It never entered Fargo's head to run or try to talk his way out of the scrape. He accepted the challenge calmly, as he would the charge of a bull buffalo or the fierce rush of a mountain lion. Squaring his shoulders, he looked for the dull glint of cold steel but saw none. They weren't out to kill him, or cut him up. They were there to beat him into the deck.

The spokesman for the quartet seemed perplexed by his silence. "Nothing to say for yourself, mate? Or are you so scared you're wettin' your britches?"

The others chuckled.

"When this is over," Fargo told them, "tell Carver he'll have to try harder next time. And not to send greenhorns to do a man's job."

That did it. Snarling deep in his chest, the foremost roustabout—or rooster, as they liked to call themselves—advanced with his scarred, knobby fists cocked. "For that I'm going to pound you to a pulp, mate."

All bluster and brute strength, the man waded in and swung a ponderous looping right that would have shattered a board had it landed. But with lithe ease, Fargo ducked under it and slammed an uppercut into the rooster's jaw that toppled the man back against his companions.

"Leave now or you'll regret it," Fargo said, offering them their one and only chance.

"Like hell!" spat another, and closed in.

The four had been clever in blowing out the nearest lamps and plunging the passageway into darkness so that no one else would notice what they were up to. But they had outfoxed themselves. Because now it was so dark, they couldn't see well enough to fight effectively.

They had also erred in their choice of spots to jump Fargo. Had they done it on the hurricane deck or any wide-open area where they had room to maneuver, they'd have had the advantage. But in the narrow confines of the passage, only one of them could attack at a time. They couldn't use their greater numbers to advantage.

Fargo braced himself as the second rooster lunged. Dodging, he flicked a one-two combination that sent the crewman reeling against the rail.

"Damn it! Get him!"

The third roustabout tried. More cautious than his friends, he moved in slowly, crouched in a boxing stance.

Fargo had to end it quickly, before it dawned on them to rush him all at once. He blocked a left hook, countered with a right, then rammed his fist into the roustabout's gut, doubling the man over. Linking his hands, Fargo swung his arms like a club and smashed the tough in the mouth, felling him where he stood.

"Enough!" roared the fourth crewman. He hurtled over his fallen shipmate and rained blows in a steady barrage, striving to batter Fargo down by sheer overpowering force.

Giving way, Fargo retreated several steps, just enough to give him room to drop into a crouch and lash out with his right boot. The crack of a knee elicited a shriek from the rooster. The man tottered, swearing luridly, and was caught flat-footed by Fargo's lightning-quick uppercut.

Two of them were down, another leaning against

the rail. The first man, the spokesman, had regained his feet but showed no inclination to try again.

"Enough?" Fargo said.

"Enough." The roustabout helped his fellows up and they departed, much against the wishes of the man whose knee was shattered. He cursed them for cowards and goaded them to finish Fargo off, but they ignored his taunts as they dragged him off.

Fargo's right hand was sore. He flexed his fingers to ensure he could draw his pistol if need be, then fished the key to his compartment from his pocket and opened the door. Typical of most, it was small and Spartan, with a bed barely big enough for an adult, an oaken stand, and a washbasin and pitcher of water.

Sliding the bolt, Fargo sank onto the creaking bed and considered whether he should confront Jace Carver over the attack. Why bother? was his conclusion. The conniving schemer would deny he'd had anything to do with it.

Stretching out, Fargo left his gunbelt and boots on in the off chance Carver or his hired men would try something else. The chug of the engine droned him to sleep, but it was a fitful rest. He tossed and turned, waking up at any unusual noise, however slight. He had about decided he was wasting his time and that he should get up and go for a stroll when the door latch jiggled.

Someone was trying to open it! Sitting bolt upright, Fargo palmed the Colt. "Who's there?" he demanded.

"Skye, it's me, Paula Simmons."

Fargo opened the door and was immediately wreathed in tantalizing perfume as the redhead slipped inside and quickly closed it behind her. She wore a long blue robe that sheathed her luscious figure like a glove, accenting her considerable charms.

"I can't let anyone spot me or I'll be in hot water. Mr. Carver would have a fit if he knew I'd snuck from my compartment."

Fargo cracked the door and checked the passageway. "I don't see anyone."

"It's past midnight. Most of the crew are below-decks, asleep." Paula leaned against the wall and ran a hand through her full mane of hair. "Mr. Carver is sawing logs, too. He drank so much wine tonight, he passed out without indulging himself with Dulcie, Tricia, or me. We were tickled pink."

"Do they know you're here?"

"No one does." Paula smiled warmly. "I couldn't sleep and wanted some company. Hope you don't mind?"

"I couldn't sleep either," Fargo said. It didn't take a genius to guess why she had come. Ordinarily, he would be on her like a bear on honey, but he had her safety to think of. "Maybe this isn't such a smart idea."

"You're throwing me out?" Paula said with a sly grin. Sashaying up to him, she placed her hands on his shoulders and lightly nibbled on his chin. "And here I thought I was doing my good deed for the day by warning you."

"Warning me of what?"

"Some crewmen came to see Carver not long after you had left. One of them had a split lip, another had a bloody nose. Carver was furious with them, and I heard him say that for two bits he'd have them thrown overboard. Then he looked at Meachum and said, 'So much for your bright idea. We'll teach him a lesson my way next time.'" Paula ran a finger over Fargo's ear. "I'm not the brightest candle in creation, but I'd stake my bottom dollar he was talking about you."

So would Fargo. All he could do about it was stay vigilant and never turn his back on anyone wearing yellow.

"So, do I get to stay?" Paula requested in a lilting voice. "Pretty please? Only for an hour or so. Then I'll traipse back to my compartment like a good little girl." Grinning, she pecked him on the neck, on the cheek, then on his earlobe.

"Behave yourself a minute," Fargo said. Her warm breath had brought goosebumps to his flesh and provoked a stirring below his belt. "I want you to talk to your friends. Convince them to stay on board when we reach the Platte."

"They'd never agree."

"Even when their lives are at stake? Trust me, Paula. They have no notion of what they're letting themselves in for. It won't be so bad on the way to Fort Kearney, but from there on, anything can happen."

The redhead ran her hands down Fargo's back to his hips. "You're sweet. But if we were to back out, Mr. Carver wouldn't pay us the money he's promised."

There it was again, Fargo reflected. The damnable money. "No amount is worth your lives."

"Mr. Carver insists we're not in any danger," Paula said. "Not with over twenty guns to guard us." Cupping his bottom she pulled him against her. "And I tend to agree. Now, enough talk. We're wasting valuable time. What's it going to be? Do I go or stay?"

Fargo's answer was to cover her soft mouth with his and glide his tongue past her raspberry lips. A low groan escaped her, the first of many to come. He undid the belt to her robe and let it swing open. A shrug on her part sent it to the floor. Underneath she wore a few skimpy undergarments, and that was all. Placing a hand on her right breast, he squeezed gently, then pinched her hardening nipple.

"Oh, yes," Paula husked. "I've wanted you since I saw you back at the house. All of us have."

It was news to Fargo, and under different circumstances he would be eager to have them prove it. But as things currently stood, he couldn't afford the distraction. Even now, as he steered the redhead toward the bed, he was listening for sounds out on deck, for any sign that more trouble was brewing. It wasn't easy to enjoy himself when he might be attacked at any moment. But he would still try.

Easing Paula down onto her back, Fargo sat beside her and drank in the vision of her ravishing loveliness.

His eyes were accustomed enough to the gloom to admire how her lustrous tresses spilled over the pillow, how her mounds arched upward with their tips as rigid as spikes.

Paula's rosy lips creased in a seductive smile, her hips moving suggestively. "What are you waiting for?"

"You're beautiful."

"Oh?" Reaching up, Paula locked her fingers behind his neck and pulled his face close to hers. "Romantic devil, aren't you? Jace Carver isn't. His idea of lovemaking is to throw a girl down, poke her for a minute or two, and then go on about his business."

"I couldn't care less what that son of a bitch does."

"Sorry," Paula said, and grinned. "Hope I didn't spoil your mood."

"Talk about something else," Fargo said. "Or, better yet, don't say anything at all." And to make sure she didn't, he kissed her again with an intensity that left her breathless. Meanwhile, his hands explored her exquisite delights, from the soft contours of her slender shoulders, to the flat of her stomach, to the thatch of curly down at the junction of her smooth thighs. She wriggled when he touched her there, her legs moving apart as his fingers slowly slid even lower.

"Lordy, you make me hot."

The feeling was mutual. Fargo's manhood was iron, bulging against his pants, in desperate need of release.

"You don't need the hardware, do you?" Paula said, unfastening his gunbelt. She set it down next to the bed, then did the same with his hat. "What about the boots and spurs?"

"Leave them on," Fargo said. As much because they didn't have a lot of time as because they might have unexpected visitors.

"Now, where were we?" the redhead teased, and pulled him down. Her body yielded to his, cushioning him, her legs snaking around his hips.

Fargo's right hand slid to her nether region, his finger tracing across her moist portal. At the contact Paula arched her spine and grasped his shoulders. She was ready for him. More than ready, for when he slowly inserted a finger, he found her inner walls were drenched.

"Ohhhhhhhhhh."

Fargo smothered her moan with his mouth, their lips fusing, their tongues meeting midway. With his other hand he massaged her breasts, taking turns with one and then the other, tweaking her nipples and flicking them between his thumb and forefinger.

Paula gripped his hair and began to grind her hips toward him. "More," she breathed.

Fargo obliged. He bent down to lather her heaving mounds from top to bottom, swirling his tongue around and around as her nails dug into his back. He sucked on a nipple, then bit it ever so lightly.

The redhead commenced panting as if she had run a mile, her hands running up and down his arms. Her eyes were hooded with pleasure, her lips as inviting as cherries. "More," she cooed. "More!"

Fargo kissed the upper swell of her bosom, then kissed and licked the base of her throat. Working up to her earlobe, he teased her ear with his deft tongue.

Paula squirmed and sighed and nipped at him with her teeth. "Don't stop. Please, don't ever stop."

Silencing her with a drawn-out kiss, Fargo caressed her inner thighs, feeling them grow warmer, feeling her shiver when his fingers brushed across her slit again. When he stroked across her swollen knob, Paula almost lifted him off the bed.

"Yesssss! There! There!"

Fargo rubbed it, each stroke inciting a spasm of pure ecstasy. Her legs clamped onto his wrist to hold it there, but they swung wide again when he suddenly lanced a finger up into her silken tunnel and followed it a fraction later with another.

The redhead's eyes grew wide and her mouth went slack. Then she humped her bottom against his hand in a raw frenzy of unchained lust. "Do me! Please, oh God please . . . do me right now!"

Fargo wasn't ready for the main course, as it were.

He pumped his fingers in and out, increasing her ardor and her need by gradual degrees rather than in a blaze of sexual hunger. Her hot mouth covered his chest with damp kisses and she began sucking on his neck, focusing on one specific spot at the nape. It sent a tingle down his back.

Lying beside her, Fargo moved his fingers ever faster, ever harder. She stopped sucking to utter a long, long moan, which grew in volume as she neared the brink. When he pressed his thumb to her knob while continuing to stroke her, she flung herself at him as if to heave him off the bed. Her arms wrapped around his shoulders and she buried her mouth in the crook of his neck, huffing like a steam engine.

Fargo's hand was molten lightning, his fingers twin pistons. His wrist started to ache from the strain and he was about to pull out when at long last he achieved the result he was striving for.

"Ahhhhhhhh! I'm there!"

That she was. Paula thrashed and bucked and bounced like a wild mare that refused to be ridden. Her legs levered upward to increase the friction and her enjoyment.

Fargo had a wildcat on his hands. He held on, stroking for as long as she heaved and gasped. When she finally subsided, he slid his fingers out, lowered his pants, and eased on top of her, his pole poised at the entrance to her garden of delights. She was in a daze, floating on a euphoric cloud, and didn't notice until he rubbed himself against her.

"Oh, God." Paula's eyes fixed on him. "You're one of the best I've ever had. I don't know if I can keep as quiet as I should."

"Scream into this," Fargo said, sliding the pillow out from under her.

Grinning, she took hold of it. "Even this might not be enough. I haven't wanted a man this much in ages."

"Thank you, ma'am," Fargo joked.

Then the time for banter was past. Fargo gripped her hips to hold them still and inched up inside her.

Paula trembled and gripped him with all her strength. When he was all the way in, she let out a long breath and whispered two words.

"So big!"

Fargo rocked on his knees, pacing himself, and fastened his mouth to her breast. She was velvet inside, smooth and wet, fitting as snugly as a glove. Soon her inner walls rippled and contracted, heightening the thrill. Abruptly stopping, he set himself and rammed up into her as if seeking to split her in half.

"Ahhhhhhh! Skye! Oh, Skye!" Paula unleashed another deluge of empassioned groans.

Again and again Fargo plunged into her. As the tempo increased, Paula's mouth sought his own and stayed there. Her hips rose to match his thrusts, her legs rising with each of his downward strokes. They were one in body, one in their goal of attaining the peak of carnal heights, and beyond.

The bed shook as if caught in a Texas twister, banging up and down, making more noise than Fargo cared for. But he didn't stop. He couldn't stop, not even if someone were battering down the compartment door. He was close now, so close. It wouldn't take much to trigger his pent-up craving.

Paula crested once again. Enfolding him in her willowy arms and legs, she sank her face into the pillow and screamed, unable to contain herself, her whole body quaking from the violence of her passion.

That did it. Fargo couldn't hold back any longer. The room blurred as he reached his own point of no control. For seconds that lasted forever, he was lost in a tidal wave of delicious sensation. His heart was thumping like a sledgehammer when at long last he coasted to a stop and lay on top of Paula, who had gone as limp as a rag doll.

"Thank you," she whispered. "I needed that."

"Any time." Fargo rolled onto his right side between the redhead and the wall, facing the door. He strained his ears but heard nothing to indicate anyone had overheard them. The walls were paper thin but he didn't think the adjoining compartments were occupied. At least he hadn't seen anyone going in or out of them before he had retired. Meachum, Banner, and Timmons were all down at the other end of the *Yellow Rose,* preferring to stay close to their boss even in sleep.

Paula shifted so they were nose to nose. "I've been thinking about what you said at supper. About how risky it is for us to tag along to Finlay's Bend."

"And?"

"I don't want to go but I can't back out. I'm sorry. Dulcie and Tricia are my friends, and they both want to see this through to the end."

"To milk Carver for as much money as they can, you mean," Fargo corrected her.

"That, too," Paula admitted. "The longer we stay with him, the more we'll make. When this is done, we'll all have tidy nest eggs socked away for the future."

"Provided you live long enough to spend it."

"Please don't be upset with us." Paula placed a hand on his chest. "Sometimes people have to do things they don't want to." Sadness etched her face. "Surely that's happened to you now and then?"

"Once or twice," Fargo conceded. Agreeing to guide Carver was a perfect example. He wanted out, he wanted to tell Carver to go to hell, but the homesteaders needed supplies to make it through the winter. And if he could prevent a clash with the fierce Pawnees, so much the better.

"Then you understand," Paula said, nuzzling against him. Closing her eyes, she hugged him and lay still, resting.

"I understand," Fargo said. She was only trying to make ends meet, the same as Smithers and Timmons and everyone else who let Carver ride roughshod over them. In that respect they were no different from most other people.

Closing his own eyes, Fargo rested his cheek on her forehead. He didn't mean to fall asleep, only to let her have a few minutes of peace and quiet. So he was all the more taken aback when loud thumping on the door woke him from a deep slumber. He sat up a second before Paula did, and when she opened her mouth to blurt something out, he covered it with his hand and whispered, "Shhhhh. Not a peep."

The thumping grew louder. "Trailsman! Open this door before I have it kicked in!"

It was Jace Carver. Fargo slid from the bed, hitched up his pants, and snatched the Colt up off the floor. Motioning for the redhead to keep quiet, he grasped her wrist and pulled her over behind the door. Only then did he throw the small bolt and open up just wide enough for him to see his visitor. "What do you want?"

Carver wasn't his usual groomed, impeccable self. His jacket was unbuttoned, his shirt hung partway out, and his hair was disheveled. Not only that, his breath reeked of wine and he swayed slightly as he shook an accusing finger. "Where's Paula Simmons?"

"How the hell should I know?" Fargo replied.

"She's not here?" Carver scratched his head. "But I was sure she would be. I saw how she was making doe eyes at you during supper."

"I don't like being woke up in the middle of the night," Fargo bluffed. "Go bother someone else."

Carver glanced down, spied the Colt, and smirked. "Or what? You'll shoot me? You're not the type."

"How would you know?" Fargo's finger was on the trigger, itching to tighten, but Carver was right. He'd never gunned anyone down in cold blood and he wasn't going to start now, no matter how much the monster deserved it.

"I can read men and women like books," the other boasted. "How do you think I've risen so high in the business world? I know what everyone is thinking, what they're feeling. It's all as plain to me as the noses on their faces." Carver puffed out his chest, pleased with himself. "It's a knack I've had since I was knee-high to a calf."

"Good for you." Fargo started to close the door but Carver stuck his foot into the opening.

"Take you, for example. You're a loner, and you like it that way. You don't back down to anyone, ever, so it galls you working for someone like me. You'd love to punch me in the teeth but you won't unless I throw the first punch, which I'm not stupid enough to do. So you're stuck counting the minutes until we reach Finlay's Bend and we part company." Carver paused. "Anything I've missed?"

"You think you have me all figured out, huh?"

"Feel free to prove me wrong whenever you want," Carver said. "Just not right this moment. I have a dove to locate." He walked off toward the bow, his hand on the wall for support.

Carver was hardly out of sight before two more forms hove out of the darkness. Both were as nattily dressed as ever, their bowlers squarely perched on their heads.

"Aren't you up a little late?" Fargo remarked.

"We're keeping an eye on Mr. Carver," Meachum stated.

"It's our duty to see he comes to no harm, even if he doesn't know we're doing it," Banner said.

Fargo watched until they had gone around a corner, then turned to discover the redhead right behind him. She had her robe on, the cotton belt knotted loosely at her slim waist. "Where do you think you're going?" he asked her.

"Aft, to the boiler deck. I'll wait there until Carver finds me," Paula said. "If he raises a fuss, I'll tell him I couldn't sleep and went for a walk on deck."

"What if he doesn't believe you?"

"Why wouldn't he? What else would I be doing?" Grinning, Paula kissed him and slipped outside. With a cheery wave she was gone, hastening in the opposite direction Carver and the other two had gone.

Against his better judgment, Fargo let her go. She had a clever head on her lovely shoulders and would be able to talk herself out of trouble. Even so, he left his door open a couple of inches and sat on the edge of the bed, listening. He figured he would wait awhile before turning in, in case there was a commotion.

And sure enough, there was.

A shout came from the port side, back near the main cabin. Fargo didn't quite catch what was said, nor did he recognize who said it. Darting to the door, he stepped into the passageway in time to glimpse someone vanish into a doorway near the other end of the riverboat. No other shouts knifed the night, and for a few seconds he thought that was the end of it.

Then, from the very rear of the vessel, from the area of the boiler deck where Paula had gone, the muggy air was rent by a piercing scream.

7

Skye Fargo ran aft almost the entire length of the *Yellow Rose* to the boiler deck, which was located above the engine room at the rear of the riverboat.

Fargo automatically assumed Paula Simmons was being beaten by Jace Carver, and he had his hand on his Colt as he sped past the last cabin. But when he burst onto the deck, the redhead was nowhere to be seen. Carver, though, was by the far railing, peering over it, and didn't notice his arrival.

Running across the deck, Fargo demanded, "Where is she?"

Carver turned, blinking, still much under the influence of the wine he had imbibed. "I didn't mean to do it!" he blurted. "I honestly didn't!"

"Do what?" Fargo asked. Even as he did, the awful truth flooded through him and he stepped to the rail and gazed down at the murky surface of the Missouri.

"We were arguing," Carver said thickly, slurring the words. "I pushed her. Not hard, I thought, but she went over the side. I tried to grab her but she fell too fast." He mopped at his sweaty brow. "I didn't see her come up again after she went under."

Fargo was already stripping off his gunbelt. As he dropped it to the deck, Meachum and Banner arrived. Tossing his hat on top of the gunbelt, Fargo sat down and started to tug at his right boot.

"What do you think you're doing?" Carver asked.

Fargo didn't answer. Every second was crucial. He yanked the right boot off and started on the left. Others had heard Paula's scream, and shouts of alarm were breaking out on both the upper and lower decks.

Carver wagged a finger at him. "You're insane! You'll be killed! I forbid you to try."

"Have Captain Trent turn the *Yellow Rose* around as soon as he can," Fargo instructed. "Light all the lamps and lanterns and have everyone man the rails and be on the lookout for us."

"Didn't you hear me?" Jace Carver practically screeched. "I forbid it! I can't let anything happen to you. I need you."

Fargo stepped to the rail and started to climb. "Bring the riverboat around," he repeated.

"How dare you ignore me!" Carver snapped, and whirled toward his underlings. "Don't let him jump!"

Meachum and Banner sprang, each seizing hold of one of Fargo's legs. They tried to tear him off the rails, but Fargo gripped the top one and clung on. Fury welled up within him, outraged that they would thwart his attempt to save a woman's life. Whipping his right elbow back and around, he slammed it full into Banner's face, knocking the man backward. Meachum still had hold of him, though, but a jab to the throat slackened Meachum's grip enough for Fargo to break free.

"Stop him!" Carver fumed. "Stop him, I say!"

Fargo clambered onto the top rail. For a heartbeat he was precariously balanced over a darkling void, then he leaped outward as far as his legs would propel him to land clear of the *Yellow Rose*. Windmilling his arms to stay upright, he dropped feet first. He had to. There was no telling how deep the water was.

Riverboats were designed so that their draft was as slight as possible. They were built to navigate extremely shallow waters by having over eighty percent of their bulk above the water line. Unloaded, a typical riverboat could sail smoothly along with as little as twenty-four inches of water under its bow. Fully loaded, the draft was about twice that.

So Fargo had no idea whether the river at that point

was two feet deep, or twenty. Had he dived headfirst into twenty inches of water, he might have crushed his skull or splintered his spine. As it was, he risked breaking both legs and suffering a paralyzing injury.

There was a rush of cool air, and Fargo smelled the dank moisture of the Missouri mixed with the acrid scent of the smoke pouring from the *Yellow Rose*'s twin chimneys. Then the dully shimmering surface broadened below him, and he took a deep breath moments before he cleaved the water like a falling rock. A cold, clammy sensation enveloped him as he shot downward into near total gloom. Ten feet. Fifteen. Twenty.

Fargo's rate of descent slowed dramatically but he was still sinking fast when he hit the bottom. It came on him so swiftly, so unexpectedly, that there was nothing he could do to prevent it. At the impact, he recoiled, thinking his legs would be snapped like kindling. Instead, to his dismay, he sank almost up to his knees in muck that had the consistency of quicksand.

Relieved, Fargo glanced upward at the riverboat's receding lights. They helped orient him. He kicked to return to the surface—but didn't budge. Thinking a little more effort would do the trick, he kicked harder. But he barely moved.

He was stuck! Fargo realized. The mud had sucked him in and was clinging fast. Unless he could loosen its grip in the next minute or two, he would drown.

Fargo wrenched to the right, then to the left. He pumped his arms for all they were worth. He churned his legs as much as he was able. With each passing second he was able to move a little bit more, but it wasn't enough for him to succeed in freeing himself. It was nowhere near enough.

Desperate, his lungs aching, Fargo struggled like a madman, thrashing and heaving upward again and again. Yet the remorseless mud refused to yield.

Suddenly tucking at the waist, Fargo dug at the muck, gouging his fingers in to the knuckles, striving to loosen it enough for him to swim off. But it was like using a thimble to bail out an ocean. For every handful he scooped out, twice as much oozed into the hole he had just created.

The torment in his lungs was growing unbearable. They were on fire, demanding air soon, or they would rupture.

In a last-ditch attempt to reduce the suction, Fargo plunged his right arm into the river bottom as far as it would go, clear down to his shoulder. Straining mightily, he worked it back and forth and felt water pour in.

Fargo couldn't hold out much longer. The impulse to open his mouth and take a breath was almost irresistible. Unfurling, he threw himself upward and stroked fiercely. Nothing happened, though.

The end was near. The river had won. It had done what grizzly bears, rattlers, stampeding buffalo, and every hostile tribe from the Plains to the Pacific Ocean had been unable to do so far, it had killed him.

More out of anger than any hope it would help, Fargo tried one last time. He flung himself upward. For a moment more the mud held, and then, wonder of wonders, he popped free, like a cork popping from a champagne bottle, propelled as if fired from a cannon.

But was it too late? Fargo's vision was clouding and his throat was constricting, a bonfire raging in his chest. Water began to seep into his mouth and his nostrils. He was on the verge of gagging, of filling his lungs with water instead of precious air, when he finally sliced through the surface.

Paddling his legs to stay afloat, Fargo gulped in breath after wheezing breath, making more noise than a steam engine. Weak from exhaustion, he would have liked to float there awhile to recover. But he couldn't. He had Paula to think of.

In the distance, to the north, glistened the sparkling lights of the *Yellow Rose*—disappearing around a bend. Apparently Carver hadn't ordered the captain to turn the vessel around.

Fargo made a vow. He promised himself that if he survived, he would hunt Jace Carver down—to the ends of the earth, if need be. And when he found him, Carver would learn there were limits to how far people could be pushed. Neither Meachum nor Banner, nor any of the guards, nor all the money in the world would save him.

Turning, Fargo paddled southward in search of the redhead. He was swimming with the current so it didn't require much energy, which was just as well since he had none to spare. "Paula?" he called out, but the only answer was the croak of a bullfrog on the eastern shore.

Fargo was afraid she was dead. The fall alone was enough to kill anyone if they landed wrong, either by breaking their neck or stunning them so they drowned. Or maybe she had wound up stuck in the muck as he had, in which case the odds of her escaping were slim to none.

"Paula?" Fargo shouted again, and every half a minute or so thereafter, hoping against hope. Bit by bit his strength returned and the ache in his chest faded. He was bitterly cold, though, bringing to mind all the tales of frontiersmen who had succumbed to the chill of many a river and lake.

Fargo tried to estimate how far the *Yellow Rose* had traveled since the redhead had fallen overboard. It hadn't taken him more than forty or fifty seconds to reach the boiler deck after hearing her scream. Allowing another sixty to ninety seconds until he dived from the rail, he guessed upward of three minutes might have elapsed. Enough time for the riverboat to have gone a couple of hundred yards.

Fargo swam a bit further, then treaded water and cupped his hands to his mouth. "Paula!" he bawled at the top of his lungs. "Paula, can you hear me?"

So faint that Fargo almost thought he was imagining it came a response, a thin, choking cry. "Paula!" he hollered, twisting his head from side to side to better pinpoint her position when she answered.

"Skye? Is that you?" She was somewhere to the west.

"I'm coming!" Fargo yelled. "Keep shouting to guide me!" He swam toward where he believed she was located, stroking powerfully, invigorated to find her alive.

Paula did as he directed and called his name over and over. Fargo was within a stone's throw of land when he spotted a long object low to the water. He thought it was a log but as he swam nearer he saw it was a partially submerged tree stump, one of the countless snags river pilots had to be on the lookout for. And lying partly across it was a slender figure who wearily lifted her head and smiled in heartfelt relief.

"Isn't it a little late to be out for a swim?" Fargo said, making light of their plight.

"I could ask you the same," she replied gamely. He sought a handhold on the stump by running his hands up over the bark until they came in contact with the stub of a broken limb. Levering higher, he hooked his elbow over a longer branch and pulled himself completely out of the water.

Paula was shivering uncontrollably, her hair in ruins, her robe open and drenched, her cotton belt whisked away by the frigid waters. She mewed like a stricken kitten when Fargo slid an arm around her waist and hoisted her so she could sit up.

"Careful, there, lover. I'm so sore I could cry."

"We need to get you on dry ground and get a fire going," Fargo said. Her skin was icy to the touch, her lips much darker than they should be. Without a source of light he couldn't say for sure, but it was his guess they had turned a deep shade of blue. "It's only another twenty feet to the bank."

Paula sagged against him. "I couldn't swim twenty inches." A cough wracked her and she vainly tugged the wet robe tighter around her in a bid to keep warm. "It's a miracle I made it this far."

"So what's another miracle, more or less?" Sliding higher, his feet propped against a limb, Fargo shifted so his back was to her. "Wrap your arms around me. I'll carry you to shore."

"I'm too heavy," Paula objected. "You'll flounder and we'll both go under."

"I can make it," Fargo insisted, raising her arms to his neck. Pressing against him, she did as he had bid her.

"Lordy, you're warm."

"Hold on tight," Fargo advised. There was a very real danger she would slip off. And although he was confident he could save her from sinking, in her condition another soaking might prove fatal.

"As tightly as I can." Paula kissed his ear with frosty lips.

"Here goes." Reaching around behind him with his right arm, Fargo clamped it about her waist. Then, easing down, he carefully lowered the two of them back into the Missouri. The water felt even colder than before, sending a shiver through him. He could only imagine the effect it was having on her nearly bare form.

As if in confirmation, the redhead gasped and clutched him harder. "Please hurry," she said, her teeth chattering. "I'm about frozen clean through."

Striking toward shore, Fargo thrust off from the stump with both feet for added momentum. He stroked once, twice, three times, and was abruptly awash as Paula's added weight started to bear him under. Sensing the calamity in the making, she screeched and attempted to fling herself back toward the stump, and safety.

"No!" Fargo bellowed, holding her fast. She stopped squirming, but in opening his mouth he had made a mistake. Water gushed into his mouth and nose, and he couldn't breathe. Even worse, he sank up to his eyebrows.

"We're going to drown!" Paula wailed.

Kicking vigorously, Fargo rose high enough to take a breath, and resumed stroking. The redhead was quaking violently. So much so, she hampered him, slowing him drastically.

They started to flounder again. Refusing to be beaten, Fargo hurled himself at the bank, which was now only eight or nine feet away. But it might as well have been fifty. For although he exerted himself to his utmost, they barely made headway. Just when he was convinced his overconfidence had cost Paula her life, his feet alighted on something solid underwater.

Straightening, Fargo gingerly groped forward, exploring with his toes. He thought it must be another stump or a submerged log, but it was actually a gravel shelf. At any instant he expected to step into a sinkhole, but they struggled to dry land without further mishap.

Gently lowering Paula, Fargo let her cheek come to rest on his shoulder. "I'll fetch some wood." He didn't have his fire steel and flint with him, or any matches, but with a couple of sticks and some kindling, he'd have a fire roaring soon enough.

"Not yet," Paula said, gluing her trembling body to his. "Just hold me. Please. I need the warmth."

She would be better off with a fire, but Fargo embraced her and stroked her sopping hair. "Just for a minute," he said.

Paula looked into his eyes. "I can never thank you enough. How did you come after me so fast? Did they let you down over the side by a rope?"

"I jumped."

"You—?" Stunned, Paula exclaimed, "But you could have been killed!"

Fargo shrugged. "Would your rather I left you behind to die? That's what Carver would have done. To cover his blame, I guess."

"It wasn't entirely his fault," Paula said. "We were arguing. He was mad I'd left my compartment so late at night, and he ordered me not to do it ever again. I got angry and pushed him. Which made him even madder, so he pushed back. Next thing I knew, I was falling over the rail."

Fargo was amazed she would even think of defending the vermin.

"It was the wine," Paula said. "He'd never have pushed me that hard if he had been sober."

"I wouldn't bet on it," Fargo said. And the wine didn't excuse Carver from trying to stop him from diving in to help her.

Paula squeezed his wrist. "Don't hold it against him. It's not worth getting your dander up."

"You don't hold your life in very high account," Fargo commented. She couldn't be sincere, he thought. Either she didn't want him tangling with Carver out of fear for his safety, or she was worried about losing her nest egg.

"Look there!" Paula exclaimed, pointing to the north.

The twin yellow glows of lanterns were moving toward them. As the lights came closer, he distinguished four men in the *Yellow Rose*'s yawl. It was a small boat used to transport passengers to and from shore, and to ferry freshly killed game to the riverboat. Two of the four were rowing. A third was in the bow, the last man aft, both holding lanterns aloft and swinging them from side to side.

Paula giggled for joy. "They're hunting for us!" She attempted to stand but her legs gave way and she collapsed against him.

"Take it nice and slow," Fargo said. Supporting her, he rose. She was still much too cold, but once she was back on board the *Yellow Rose* they could quickly remedy that. Waving an arm, he hailed the searchers. "Over here! On the bank! Watch out for a stump close to shore!"

The man in the bow barked a command and the yawl promptly angled toward them. "Mr. Fargo? Is the woman with you? Is she all right?" the man called out.

"That's Captain Trent," Paula said. "He has such a darling southern accent."

Following the captain's instructions, the rowers skillfully brought the yawl to rest against the shore and the captain jumped out.

"My dear Miss Simmons! Thank the Lord you're all right! Mr. Carver told me about your unfortunate accident." Legitimately concerned, Trent clasped Paula's hand. "You really shouldn't fool around on the rails as you were doing."

"How's that?" Fargo said.

Trent looked at him. "Mr. Carver explained how she was a little tipsy and climbed up on the rails for the fun of it. Most unwise. They're there for a purpose, you know."

Fargo simmered with resentment. So that was the story Carver was spreading to hide what he had done! The redhead could set everyone straight and expose Carver for the bald-faced liar he was, but would she? Which was more important to her? The money she was due—or the truth?

"Yes, it was awfully foolish of me, wasn't it?" the redhead replied, giving Fargo the answer. "I'm terribly sorry to have been such a bother to everyone, Captain."

"Nonsense," Trent gallantly responded. "These things happen. But I trust you've learned to confine your shenanigans to inside the cabin from now on?"

"Oh, most assuredly," Paula said.

Fargo was eager to confront Carver. "She's half frozen. We've got to get her back quickly."

"Without delay," Captain Trent declared. Turning to the roosters, he barked, "Yarrow! Lawson! Give me your coats." The men obeyed without question, and Trent handed them to Paula, who bundled herself in both, shivering the whole while.

With the captain's aid, Fargo helped her onto the yawl. One of the rowers used his oar to push the boat toward deeper water, and within moments they were stroking northward, hugging the shore where the current was weak. Captain Trent stood in the bow, watching for obstacles.

Paula was hunched forward, her body shaking worse

than ever. "You'd think I'd be a smidgen warmer by now."

"I've seen men die after only a couple of minutes in cold water," Trent mentioned. "You're to be commended on faring so well."

"Why didn't you turn the *Yellow Rose* around instead of taking the time to lower the yawl?" Fargo asked.

"Remember that stump?" the captain said. "According to my charts, this stretch of the river is loaded with snags. The only clear channel for a vessel our size is in the middle. Wide enough for a riverboat's passage, but if I'd tried to bring her about, there was an excellent chance I'd have staved in her hull or stranded her."

Fargo couldn't blame Trent for doing what he had done. Dozens of riverboats were lost each year in that very fashion.

The captain had continued. "As soon as Mr. Carver notified me, I ran to the wheelhouse and ordered the engines stopped and the anchor dropped. We're just around the bend yonder."

That they were, the *Yellow Rose* ablaze with lights, her crew and passengers lining the rails awaiting the outcome. At the appearance of the yawl, a mate hollered down to ask if Paula was all right, and on being informed by the captain that she was, a general cheer went up, with much clapping and whistling.

Fargo didn't share in the festive spirit. After the yawl was brought alongside the larger boat, he gave Paula a boost up into the waiting arms of crew members vying for the honor of lifting her on deck. He climbed up next. Roosters were packed a dozen deep, with more hurrying from the upper deck and from aft.

"Out of our way! Move! Give Mr. Carver room!"

Meachum and Banner were shouldering their way through the throng, clearing a space for their employer. They were none too considerate about it, either, earning glares from the roustabouts. Timmons was with them but he stood well back, letting them do all the shoving.

As the crewmen parted, Jace Carver advanced, flanked by his armed guards. He was smiling at Paula Simmons, who was so worn out it took two roosters to hold her up. "Paula, my dear! You don't know how happy I am to see you safe after your unfortunate accident!" He put a hand on her shoulder. "Bring her to my cabin, men. I'll attend to her personally."

Then Fargo hit him. Taking a step, he punched Carver flushed on the jaw. The blow knocked Carver back against Meachum and Banner, who tottered but kept him from falling.

Some of the guards leveled their Spencers and might have fired had Paula not stepped in front of them. "Please, Skye," she whispered. "Don't make an issue of it. For my sake."

Fargo almost brushed her aside and advanced toward Carver anyway. There was only so much arrogance he would abide.

"Please," Paula repeated.

Carver had straightened and was rubbing his chin. His lieutenants had their hands under their jackets but before they could unlimber their hardware he declared, "No! There will be no gunplay!" Carver jabbed a finger at his guards. "That applies to you, as well! Lower your weapons."

Confused, they nonetheless obeyed.

"Mr. Fargo and I had a little misunderstanding a while ago," Carver said loud enough for everyone to hear. "He was merely venting his spleen just now. But it won't happen again, will it, Trailsman?"

Thoroughly disgusted, Fargo planted himself in front of Jace Carver. "It better not or there will be hell to pay. Savvy?"

"Is that a threat?"

"Take it any damn way you like," Fargo said, hoping Carver would be rash enough to take a swing at him. But he enjoyed no such luck.

"Let's chalk the whole thing up to too much wine

and let it go at that, shall we? A tragedy has been narrowly averted, for which we're all grateful. Now we must get on about our business."

Captain Trent's southern upbringing picked that moment to assert itself. "Gentlemen, please. While you stand here squabbling, the young lady is trembling like a leaf. We should attend to her welfare before all else."

"Without any help from you," Fargo told Carver. "You've already done enough for one night." His arm around Paula, he ushered her toward the companionway just as the other doves bustled down.

Dulcie and Tricia rushed to their friend and embraced her, both besieging her with questions.

"Take her to her room and prepare a warm bath," Fargo directed them. "She can tell you all about it then." Pausing, he glanced at the cause of it all. Carver's green eyes mirrored pure hatred. So did those of Meachum and Banner.

Fargo was under no illusions. When he had served his purpose, at the very second his usefulness to Jace Carver ended, he was a marked man.

8

The Platte River was one of many tributaries that fed into the muddy Missouri. Far less wide, and much more shallow, it wasn't navigable by any craft larger than a bullboat. At the height of the fur trade, trappers from the distant Rockies had routinely used it, but when the beaver trade died, so did the Platte's usefulness.

Then the migration West started, with thousands flocking to the goldfields of California and the lush Willamette Valley in Oregon. Since the Platte flowed year-round, unlike some waterways that dried up during the hot summer months, and since the surrounding lowlands were rife with game, the river became the main artery settlers followed across the plains.

Skye Fargo had traveled its winding length many times, but it wasn't the only route he ever took to reach the mountains. He knew the prairie, as the old saw went, like the back of his hand. He knew the course of each stream, the location of every spring. Given a choice, he often took a more direct route. But this time, he had no choice.

Now, with the morning sun warming his face, Fargo sat astride the Ovaro near a rutted track that paralleled the Platte, wishing there were a faster way to reach the four new settlements.

Jace Carver's party was mounting up except for one guard, who was busy checking the packs on their six pack animals. Below the knoll they were on, tied up at shore, was the *Yellow Rose*. All hands were on deck to see them off, while Captain Trent watched from the wheelhouse.

"At last!" Carver crowed. Attired in a riding outfit with a narrow-brimmed silk hat, he sat on a splendid bay that couldn't stand still. Prancing and bobbing its head, it was chomping at the bit to be off. "The first leg of our journey is over."

Timmons didn't appear particularly pleased about the fact. He was on a skittish sorrel, his expression and posture evidence he didn't have much experience on horseback.

Smithers, however, was handling his buttermilk horse as if born to the saddle. The butler was an unending bundle of surprises.

As for the three ladies, they were all on mares, all laughing and treating the next leg of their trek as a great lark. Paula, who had fully recovered, behaved as if nothing out of the ordinary had ever occurred. Even more mystifying, she had been hanging on Carver's elbow during daily promenades on deck, treating him no differently than she had before he pushed her in the river.

If Fargo lived to be a hundred, he would never fully understand women.

Carver brought the bay over beside the Ovaro. "Whenever you're ready, Trailsman, take the lead. I want to reach the fort as quickly as possible." He had been treating Fargo decently enough since the other night, but the act didn't fool Fargo for one minute. "I've informed everyone that they straggle at their own peril. I won't suffer a delay for anyone."

Fargo rose in the stirrups. Most of them were looking in his direction so now was as good a time as any to enlighten them on a few points. "If you start to fall behind, give a yell," he said to annoy Carver. "No firing a gun unless in an emergency. Ride single file or in pairs but don't bunch up."

"Why not?" Banner interrupted. "The trail is wide enough for all of us to ride in one group. What possible difference can it make?"

"In a group you're easier to pick off."

"You mean to say we might encounter hostiles this far east, sir?" Smithers asked, gazing all around.

The odds were slim but the possibility did exist, and Fargo assured them as much.

Carver, of course, scoffed. "Most of those red devils would think twice about attacking us, as many guns as we have."

"That cuts two ways," Fargo said. "Some tribes, like the Blackfeet, count stealing a gun as highly as they do stealing a horse. They would jump us just to *get* our weapons." Reining the pinto stallion westward, he tapped his spurs against its sides. "Move on out!"

Several blasts of the *Yellow Rose*'s whistle rolled off across the grassland, courtesy of Captain Trent, who smiled and waved in parting.

Fargo trotted on some fifty yards ahead, as much as a precaution against an ambush as to fight shy of Carver's company. The twitter of sparrows, the cry of a circling hawk, and the gurgling of the sluggish Platte all served to remind him how much he had missed the wilderness. The plains and the mountains were his true home, not the man-made confines of Kansas City or any other town.

Civilization was like medicine, Fargo mused, best taken in small doses. A week here, a week there, maybe an entire month on those rare occasions when he had enough money and a particularly pleasing companion to while away the hours with. But he always returned to the wilds. Or rather, he was drawn to them like iron to a magnet.

More than anything, Fargo valued his freedom. True freedom. The ability to do as he saw fit, when he saw fit. A man was too confined back East, where everything a person did was governed by a legion of laws, rules, and regulations.

Fargo liked his whiskey. He liked playing cards. He liked wild women. But there were people who frowned on all three, folks who figured that if they didn't approve of something or other, then no one should be allowed to indulge in it. Temperance movements had sprung up to abolish alcohol. Prim and proper citizens were pushing to make gambling illegal. And as for wild women, the mere topic was taboo in most circles.

What was it about some people, Fargo asked himself, that they thought they had the God-given right to force their will on everyone else? Which brought Jace Carver to mind.

Fargo had reached a decision. Somehow, in some way, he planned to put an end to Carver's days of pushing people around, of treating them as puppets on strings, of using his enormous wealth to buy their very souls.

The clomp of hooves to the rear brought an end to Fargo's reverie. When he saw who it was, he smiled. "Tired of your lord and master's company?"

Smithers slowed the buttermilk to the same brisk walk as the pinto, and chuckled. "I told him that I needed to find out if you would prefer brandy or whiskey with your supper this evening?"

Fargo hoped he hadn't heard correctly. As much as he liked a good, stiff drink, liquor was a surefire invitation for trouble with an outfit as green behind the ears as Carver's. To say nothing of the bloodbath they would invite should watchful hostiles discover they had it. Some Indians would kill for the white man's firewater. "How much did your boss bring?"

"A case of each. And a third case containing Scotch." The butler swatted at a bee buzzing close to his head, then said by way of explanation, "Four of Carver's hired guards are Scotsmen."

"Anything else on those packhorses I should know about?"

"Just Mr. Carver's usual provisions. Clothes, shoes, a set of fine china, silverware, and crystal glasses, cashmere blankets and silk sheets for his bedding—"

Flabbergasted, Fargo cut Smithers off. "China? Silverware? Silk *sheets*?"

"Mr. Carver insists on traveling in lavish style, sir.

As it is, he's brought only what he considers the bare necessities."

"The man is an idiot," Fargo said flat-out.

"True. However, he's an extremely rich idiot. So it behooves us lesser mortals to indulge his idiocy or pay for our folly."

"Did he remember to bring extra ammunition?" Which, to Fargo's way of thinking was more essential than anything else.

"Oh, yes, sir. Plenty. Including several spare rifles and pistols, and a keg of black powder."

Fargo couldn't see why Carver had brought black powder when the guards' Spencers and pistols relied on ready-made cartridges. It made no sense. But then, neither did much else Jace Carver did.

"He also brought a box of nuts imported from the Middle East, his favorite jam, and several cartons of eggs."

"What, no caviar?" Fargo asked sarcastically.

"Actually, sir, yes. Along with salted crackers." Smithers sighed. "It took me three days to pack everything."

"When you get back to Kansas City, you owe it to yourself to find someone else to work for," Fargo said.

"I tend to agree, but I didn't ride up here to discuss Mr. Carver or myself," Smithers revealed. "I came to give you another warning. Last night I overheard something that leads me to believe a plot has been hatched to eliminate you."

"I'm all ears."

Before the butler could share the details, more hooves drummed behind them. Jace Carver and his executive assistants rode up, Carver stating, "It takes you this long to ask a simple question, Smithers? You could have told him your life's story by now."

"Sorry, sir. We were making small talk, is all."

"Ride back and join the rest," Carver commanded. "I don't want you distracting our scout. You heard him say we might run into hostiles. He needs to keep alert."

"As you wish, sir," Smithers dutifully said, and left.

Carver looked at Fargo. "Any objections?"

"He's your butler."

"Everyone here is in my employ, in one way or another," Carver responded. "You would do well to remember that. And to keep your mind on your work. So far I've been willing to tolerate your lapses, but from here on out I require that you do your job with the utmost efficiency."

"Don't push it," Fargo said.

But Carver didn't know when to shut up. "I hardly think I'm being unreasonable. Not when all our lives are in your hands."

"I'm the best there is at what I do, remember?" Fargo said. "Weren't those your own words?"

"And I hope to heaven your reputation is well deserved," Carver replied. "Between the Pawnees and other threats, there's no telling when we'll be set upon."

Fargo assumed he was referring to other hostile tribes, or maybe bears and cougars and other beasts of the wild. "I've dealt with them all before. I'll get you through to Finlay's Bend."

"I hope so. Just don't take anything for granted. Not anything." With that puzzling comment, Carver and his shadows dropped back to rejoin the main party.

Fargo had been sincere. He would do all in his power to protect them. Not for Carver's sake, obviously. Or for Meachum's and Banner's, or for any of the hired guns. They could ride off a cliff, for all he cared. No, he'd do it for the sake of the three women, and for Smithers. For Timmons, too, since the mousy little secretary had always treated him with respect.

The remainder of the day was uneventful. Fargo shot a buck toward evening, and shortly thereafter called a halt on a grassy strip at the water's edge. Sentries were posted. The horses were taken to drink, then tethered. While everyone else sat around two campfires complaining about how sore they were after eight hours in the saddle, Fargo butchered the deer and soon had a haunch roasting over the flames.

Fargo doubted that Jace Carver would share any of his private stock of food, and he was right. Although Carver partook of the venison, he also treated himself to delicacies fit for a royal table. Smithers was made to attend his every whim.

Along about ten, the camp quieted. Fargo advised them to turn in early as they were heading out the next morning at the crack of dawn, and Carver turned the advice into an order, instructing everyone to bed down immediately. True to form, no one protested.

By ten-thirty Fargo was the only one still up, except for a pair of guards. Which was fine by him. He sat sipping coffee until midnight, enjoying the peaceful prairie night. Other than the occasional yip of a coyote, all was quiet.

Before first light Fargo was awake and had the Ovaro saddled. He set two fresh pots of coffee brewing before anyone else cracked an eyelid, and the fragrant aroma awoke Carver, who proceeded to rouse everyone else by walking from blanket to blanket and nudging them with a toe.

While the ladies went off in the bushes, the men prepared to head out once breakfast—which consisted of leftover venison—was finished. Carver had Smithers make him a few rolls smeared in jam, and laced his coffee with a splash of brandy.

By the time a rosy crown adorned the eastern horizon, they were under way. Once again Fargo rode well ahead of the others. No one came up to join him, not even Smithers or Paula, leading him to suspect Carver had forbid it.

At midday Fargo called for a short halt. He wanted to get the butler alone for a minute to ask about the plot he'd mentioned, but Carver kept Smithers close to his side. Again, Fargo wondered if it was deliberate.

That evening was more of the same. No one said two words to him. Smithers never left Carver's side, while Paula was always kept to the company of Dulcie and Tricia.

Fargo didn't let it bother him. They were the ones who refused to do anything to jeopardize their positions, who valued money more than their pride. They had to live with the consequences, not him. And in a way, he liked being left to himself. There were less headaches that way.

The next several days were identical. Everyone settled into a routine, and all went well.

Then came a blustery afternoon, with the wind gusting from the northwest and a hint of rain in the air. Fargo saw thunderclouds to the north but believed the storm would miss them. In case it didn't, he called an early halt in a belt of cottonwoods. While some of the guards collected dead limbs for firewood and others tended to the horses, Fargo cradled his Henry and stalked into the woods in search of game for the supper pot.

Most of the wildlife was lying low. Fargo hiked over a mile before he spotted anything worthwhile, a large rabbit which he dropped with a shot to the head. Further along he spied a doe but it bounded off as he was taking a hasty bead. Another rabbit was the best he could do.

Twilight had claimed the prairie when Fargo made his way back. Out of habit, he moved as silently as a Comanche, his senses primed. So when he registered movement where there shouldn't be any, he instinctively hunkered and tucked the Henry's stock to his shoulder.

A man on a dun was spying on the camp. It was the steady flick of his mount's tail that had caught Fargo's eye. The rider was in his thirties and dressed in homespun clothes. Other than an old hunting rifle in a saddle scabbard, he didn't appear to be armed.

Rising, Fargo approached from the rear, the blustery wind ensuring that even if he were to mistakenly step on a twig, the man wouldn't hear anyway. When he was only a few yards behind the dun, he stopped. "You can join us, if you'd like."

The rider twisted so abruptly, he nearly fell from his saddle. He had a pudgy, tanned face, and a couple weeks' worth of whiskers. "Tarnation, mister! You plumb scared me to death!"

Fargo moved next to the horse, which was lathered with sweat, a sign it had been ridden long and hard. "I'm guiding those people you were watching," he said.

For a second the man seemed ready to slap his legs against the dun and bolt. But thrusting out a calloused hand, he introduced himself. "Tom Johnson. I'm on my way to Kansas City and happened to see the fire."

"Why didn't you ride on in?" Fargo asked, shaking hands. On the frontier it was customary for fellow travelers to be made welcome.

Johnson frowned. "I was working up the courage. I'm a mite skittish around other folks. Or as my wife likes to say, I'm too darned shy for my own good."

"You have a family?"

"Sure do," Johnson said with pride. "We're farming a section out near Grinder Hollow. Two hundred acres, all our own."

"Where?"

"A new settlement about forty miles west of Fort Kearney," Johnson said. "It's not much to speak of— only about ten families and a small store."

"I've heard there were some new settlements that way," Fargo mentioned.

"Four, to be exact. Grinder Hollow is closest to the post. Then there's Willow, Platteville, and Finlay's Bend. Farming communities, mainly. But in another ten years they'll all be full-fledged towns."

They might be, Fargo mused. Provided they weren't wiped out by Indians or fell prey to drought, a prairie fire, or some other disaster. Settlements sprang up all the time, only to fade as swiftly as the morning dew. "Join us. We have coffee to spare."

Johnson glanced toward the camp and bit his lower

lip. "I reckon it'll be all right. I don't want to impose, though."

"Consider yourself my guest," Fargo said to put him at ease.

One of the guards was the first to spot them and hiked his rifle, lowering it again when he recognized Fargo.

Jace Carver heard the dun, glanced over a shoulder, then shot to his feet, almost spilling a crystal glass of whiskey. As was usually the case, Meachum, Banner, Timmons, and the women were all seated around the same fire, and when Carver jumped up, so did his two assistants.

"Who's that with you, Fargo, and what in hell is he doing here?"

Fargo introduced the farmer, explaining where he was from, and saying, "He's on his way to Kansas City. All he wants is some coffee." Stepping to his bedroll, Fargo rummaged in his saddlebags for his battered tin cup, then started to look for one for the farmer. Turning, he discovered Johnson was still in the saddle, nervously being studied by Carver and the other two. "Climb on down," he said.

"Not so fast," Carver rasped. "How do we know we can trust him?"

"He's a farmer, not a Pawnee," Fargo pointed out. "What do you expect him to do? Pull a plow from his pocket and beat you to death?"

The women giggled, which Carver's didn't like one bit. "Don't be flippant. A man in my position can't be too cautious."

Tom Johnson fidgeted. "Look, I don't want to be a bother, mister. If you don't want me here, I'll go."

"Oh, hell." Fargo strode past Carver and gripped the dun's bridle. "You'll do no such thing. Step down and stay a spell." It gave him no small pleasure to buck Carver, who looked fit to be tied.

Apprehensive, Johnson slid off his mount. "For a while, I reckon. But I don't want to make anyone mad."

"You mean him?" Fargo said, nodding at Carver. "He was born mad."

Carver flared like a torch. "Need I remind you who's in charge? From here on out, no one is to be brought into camp without my specific permission. You don't realize what's at stake." Spinning on their visitor, he said, "Do you have any idea who I am?"

"No, sir," Johnson said meekly.

"Frisk him," Carver told Meachum and Banner, and the pair moved toward the farmer from either side.

Scared, Johnson poked both arms into the air and bleated, "I'm not carrying a gun! Honest! All I've got is a rifle. It's on my horse."

Banner ran a hand under Johnson's woolen jacket and patted his pockets. "He's telling the truth, sir," he reported.

To Fargo, Carver's behavior was becoming more bizarre by the day. Anyone with eyes could see that Tom Johnson was exactly what he claimed to be, and as harmless as a kitten. He took a china cup from among those Carver's people were using and filled it. "Here's that coffee I promised you, Tom."

Johnson slowly lowered his hands and accepted it. "Thank you, most kindly. Truth is, I haven't eaten or drank much of anything the past week. Ever since I got word my sister is awful sick. At death's door, the letter said."

"This is the furthest you've ridden in a week?" Carver asked, as suspicious as ever. "You could have been almost to Kansas City if you pushed yourself night and day."

"And ride my horse into the ground?" Johnson said. "Mister, where I come from, they don't exactly grow on trees. Besides, I didn't get started until three days ago. It took me a while to arrange things so my neighbors could help my missus out if need be." He tilted the cup to his lips. "Say, this is right tasty. I ain't ever had coffee like this before. Where did it come from?"

Smithers was standing at a small folding table across

the fire, spreading fresh butter on a thick slice of bread. "That would be my doing, sir. I added a dash of chicory for flavoring."

Paula patted a spot beside her and her friends. "Have a seat, Mr. Johnson. Tell us all about your poor sister."

Fargo filled his own cup and moved to one side to skin and clean the rabbits. When he was finished, he dropped the chunks of meat into a large black pot, filled the pot with water, and hung it on a tripod over the fire. "Rabbit stew tonight," he explained when Smithers arched an eyebrow.

"With Mr. Carver's permission, perhaps I can add a little flavoring to it, too," the butler said, and walked over to where Carver, Meachum, and Banner were huddled. In due course he came back to the fire with a couple of tin canisters.

"More chicory?" Fargo said.

"With *rabbit*?" Smithers was positively appalled. "Mercy me, no. That would be a culinary faux pas of the first magnitude. I was thinking more along the lines of dried onions and carrots." He added spoonfuls of both and a heady aroma soon filled the clearing.

Most of the guards gathered around, as hungry as starving wolverines. But it was another quarter of an hour before the stew was done. Dulcie volunteered to ladle it out, to the guards' further delight.

The remainder of the evening went smoothly. After everyone ate, Carver wanted some entertainment and called on Timmons to recite poetry. The mousy man refused, out of embarrassment, but he changed his mind when Carver threatened to dock him a month's wages.

So it was that Fargo found himself sitting under a sparkling canopy of stars in the middle of the vast plains, listening to a man with a squeaky voice recite selected verses from *Childe Harold's Pilgrimage*.

Next Carver had Tricia sing a few bawdy tunes. It was hard to say whether her off-key voice or the jiggle of her huge breasts as she warbled was the main appeal.

Jace Carver had become a stickler for turning in at ten sharp. When he stood up and announced, "Bedtime, everyone!" every member of his party rose to turn in as meekly as sheep being turned into a holding pen.

"What about him, sir?" Banner asked, nodding at Tom Johnson.

Looking at the farmer, Carver said, "I suppose it's all right for you to spend the night with us. Spread out your bedding over there." He pointed at a spot a dozen yards from where everyone else would be sleeping.

"Thank you, sir. I'm grateful," Johnson said.

Fargo and the farmer were the only ones who stayed up, not counting a guard posted by the tethered horses and another by a tree bordering the sea of waving grass.

It wasn't long before snoring broke out. Johnson gazed at the bundled figures, then commented, "Quite a strange bunch of people you're hooked up with, Mr. Fargo, if you don't mind my saying so."

"They're city folk."

"Ah." Johnson polished off his cup of coffee. "Well, I reckon I'll be sawing logs, too. I want to get an early start. I hope to be in Kansas City by next Wednesday."

It was another hour before Fargo crawled under his own blankets. All the coffee he had drunk took a toll, though, and he couldn't get to sleep. When he finally did, it wasn't for long. Again and again he woke up, growing drowsier each time, so drowsy that when he awakened for the tenth time in the middle of the night, he couldn't make up his mind whether what he was seeing was real or a fragment of a fitful dream.

Tom Johnson was on his hands and knees, stealthily moving toward Jace Carver. And clutched in his right hand was a knife.

9

In the few seconds it took Skye Fargo to realize he was indeed awake, and that the mild-mannered farmer from Grinder Hollow was about to pounce on Jace Carver, Tom Johnson had narrowed the gap to several yards. The cold steel Johnson held glittered dully in the glow of the fire's embers.

It occurred to Fargo that all he had to do was lie there and do nothing and Jace Carver would die. But as much as Fargo disliked the man—and he had rarely disliked anyone more—it went against his grain to see another person brutally murdered, no matter how much they deserved it.

So when the farmer suddenly pushed erect and swept the knife overhead for a killing stroke, Fargo surged up out of his blankets, shouting, "Carver! Look out!"

Startled by the outcry, Tom Johnson paused and glanced toward him. It bought Jace Carver precious moments to snap awake, take in what was happening, and frantically roll to his right.

"No!" Tom Johnson wailed, slicing his blade downward. He missed Carver, the knife shearing into Carver's blanket, instead. Pivoting, Johnson thrust, but Carver scrambled out of harm's way.

Fargo dashed toward them. Others were leaping up, some with guns, and Fargo wanted to disarm the farmer before anyone squeezed off a shot.

Carver had gained his feet and was stumbling backward as Johnson came at him with a savage vengeance, slashing and swinging in a wild attempt to disembowel and slay. One of the women screamed. Curses sprinkled the night. Then Carver tripped and fell onto his back.

Aglow with triumph, Tom Johnson loomed above him and raised the knife one more time. Carver was at his mercy and they both knew it.

"No! Don't!" Jace Carver begged.

"Die, you fiend! Die!" Johnson shrieked, plunging the knife down.

Fargo only had one more stride to take when a burly guard blundered directly into his path. They collided, and although Fargo didn't go down, it proved a costly delay.

A revolver boomed twice. At each blast, Tom Johnson was jolted as if by invisible fists. Fargo saw Banner taking aim to fire a third time, and leaping, he swatted at Banner's wrist just as the Remington discharged. The slug meant for the farmer tore into the ground.

"What the hell!" Banner blurted.

Four or five others were about to fire.

"No more shooting!" Fargo shouted. "Not by anyone!"

Johnson was on his side, a scarlet stain spreading on the front of his homespun shirt, his mouth opening and closing like that of a fish out of water. He was trying to grasp his knife, which lay several inches beyond his reach. Tears of frustration filled his eyes, and he groaned. "So close. I was so close."

Fargo sank onto a knee and rolled the farmer onto his back. "Why did you try to kill Carver?"

Blood trickled from a corner of Johnson's mouth. His eyes roved upward, unfocused, as he continued to gulp air. "Hell spawn . . ." he sputtered. "Sucking life from everyone. Sucking us dry . . ."

Some of Jace Carver's bodyguards were helping him stand. "Finish the bastard off!" he snarled.

Banner made a move as if to obey but halted when Fargo glared.

Tom Johnson suddenly flailed his arms. "Don't let . . . don't let . . ." he exclaimed in a failing voice, rising a hand's width off the ground. His fingers closed on Fargo's shoulder and for a heartbeat they locked eyes, Johnson's own clear and bright. "Tell them I'm sorry I failed. I tried my best." With that, the farmer expired.

Carver stalked over. "Why did you stop Banner from killing him?" he demanded. "It's what the yokel was trying to do to me."

"What do you think was his reason?" Fargo responded. It was insane. If everything Johnson had told them was true, Johnson was a family man, a devoted husband, a hard worker who eked out a living tilling the soil. Hardly the sort of person to go around mindlessly murdering others.

"How the hell should I know?" Carver said. "You heard him, raving on about fiends and hell spawn. The man was a lunatic."

"He didn't act like one last night," Fargo observed.

Carver smoothed his rumpled nightshirt. "This is what we get for allowing a stranger into our camp. From now on, no one is to spend the night with us. I don't care who they are." He gestured at his guards. "Bury this scum."

"Hold it." Fargo checked in each of Johnson's pockets. In one he found three dollars and twenty cents, which was all the money the man had on him. In another he found a folding knife with a cracked wooden grip. And in the farmer's shirt pocket was a folded sheet of paper which Fargo opened.

"What's that you have there?" Carver inquired.

It was a letter. Fargo read it aloud. " 'Dearest Martha. If you get this it means I failed and the demon is still alive. All our prayers were for nothing. But don't be discouraged. The good Lord, in His loving wisdom, won't let us down. We have endured so much, I know, but there is light at the end of the tunnel. Carver will die, if not by my hand, then by whoever draws the short straw next.' " Fargo looked up. "He knew you?"

"Maybe he heard of me. Many have. But I never met the man."

Fargo resumed reading. " 'I've waited at the fort for over a week now. The wagons are already here. Last night I talked to one of Carver's men and he let slip that Carver is due to arrive soon. I'll head out tomorrow morning and see if I can meet them on the trail.' " Again Fargo stopped. "He was hunting you down."

"A lunatic," Carver repeated.

Fargo went on to the end. " 'Come what may, dear Martha, know that I love you with all my heart and soul. Give our children a hug and remind them of how much I cared for them. And don't forget—' " Fargo lowered the paper. "That's where it stops."

"Give it to me," Carver said, reaching out.

"Nothing doing." Folding it, Fargo slid the letter into his own pocket.

Banner stepped in front of him menacingly. "You heard Mr. Carver. Do as he tells you, mister, and fork the damn thing over."

Fargo couldn't say what made him explode. Maybe it was pent-up anger. Maybe it was the fact he was sick and tired of being told what he could and couldn't do. Maybe it was a reaction to the farmer's death. Maybe it was a combination of all three. He drove his left fist into Banner's stomach even as he straightened, his right hand on the Colt and clearing leather before anyone else could think to butt in.

Banner started to double over. The pistol butt flashed once, then twice, slamming him across the temple, and he dropped like a ten-ton boulder.

Whirling toward the guards, Fargo covered them. "Anyone else?"

All eyes shifted to Jace Carver, who appeared on the verge of throwing a tantrum. His teeth clenched, he hissed like a sidewinder about to strike. His whole body shook from the violence of his emotions, then he stood stock-still and grated, "Insult piled on insult, Trailsman. But this is the last one I'll tolerate."

Meachum had moved to Banner's side. "Say the word, Mr. Carver, and I'll dispose of him for you."

His hand was next to the flap of his jacket, his fingers curled to draw.

"That won't be necessary," Carver said, much to Meachum's disappointment. "Help Mr. Banner over to the fire and we'll tend his bruises."

The guards were lowering their rifles so Fargo lowered the Colt, shoving it back into its holster. Backing off, he sat on his blankets to ponder the latest incident.

A whole new element had been added to an already complex mystery. There was much more to Carver's trek to the settlements than Carver was letting on. Judging by the letter, the settlers at Grinder Hollow saw him as some sort of evil ogre. They despised him so much, they wanted him dead. Simple farmers, no less, who normally would never harm another living soul.

Why? The question seared Fargo like a red-hot poker. Why would they do such a thing to the man who supplied their settlement with the provisions they needed to go on running their farms? What could Carver have done to inspire so much hatred? Sure, Carver was a conceited, selfish jackass. And sure, Fargo had wanted to shoot him a couple of times himself. But farmers were basically decent, kindhearted people who always turned the other cheek when they were wronged.

One thing was for sure: Whatever Jace Carver had done, it had to be something especially vile. Something so awful, so terrible, that a loving family man like Tom Johnson had been willing to brave never seeing his loved ones again to track Carver down and kill him.

Fargo saw two guards dragging Johnson's body toward the cottonwoods, a third bearing a shovel. Smithers was rekindling the fire. Jace Carver had taken a seat next to it, a cashmere blanket draped over his shoulders. "What aren't you telling me?" Fargo asked him.

"I beg your pardon?"

"Why was Johnson sent to kill you?"

"That letter was the raving of a madman. But even if weren't, how should I know? Perhaps someone put him up to it. A man in my position makes a lot of enemies."

Suddenly Fargo recalled the comment Carver had made back at the Missouri about "the Pawnees and other threats." At the time, he'd thought it referred to hostiles or wild animals. Now he saw it differently. "You knew some of the settlers were out to get you, didn't you? That's why you've brought so many guards, and why you have more men waiting at the fort."

Carver scrunched his face up as if he had just sucked on a lemon. "How many times must I tell you the same thing? It's all as new to me as it is to you. My men are a precaution against the Pawnees, and that's all."

Fargo would believe him when cows could fly. But he didn't press it. Carver wouldn't ever admit the truth.

Everyone was too excited to go back to sleep. They ringed the fire, rubbing their hands to keep warm, anxious for the coffee to brew. Several times Fargo caught Dulcie glancing at him as if she wanted to say something but she never did.

Nerves were further frayed when a dozen or so wolves appeared in the nearby woods, possibly lured by the scent of freshly spilled blood. Their slanted eyes gleamed bright, reflected in the firelight as they paced amid the trees.

The breeze bore their scent to the horses, and many commenced to prance and nicker nervously.

"Shouldn't we drive the pack off?" a guard anxiously asked, fingering his Spencer.

"Leave them be," Fargo said. "They rarely attack people."

In the next moment there was a crash in the brush and out raced the three men who had been given the burial detail. Their rifles leveled, they retreated toward the circle of firelight. "A couple of those critters growled and came at us!" one reported.

"We didn't shoot for fear the rest would attack!" said the man at his elbow.

Fargo pushed erect. "Did you finish burying Johnson?"

"How could we?" the third man said. "Wolves were all around us, moving closer and closer. We got out of there not a moment too soon."

"Damn." Snagging the Henry, Fargo levered a round into the chamber and sprinted from the clearing. Carver bellowed for him to stop but he wasn't about to.

Wolves had gathered up ahead. A pair of human legs jutted from the cluster. Growling and shouldering one another, they tore at the farmer's body.

Fargo banged a shot into the soil. Half the wolves streaked off into the brush but the rest were too hungry to abandon their meal. Tapered teeth sheared into yielding flesh, and crunched hard onto bone.

Sighting on a wolf that had Johnson by the throat, Fargo cored its chest. He thought it would be enough to convince the others to flee but only two more did, leaving three who weren't about to forsake their feast.

Slowing ten feet from their dusky forms, Fargo fired again. A wolf arced high into the air, yowling lustily, then sprawled across the farmer and broke into frenzied convulsions. That did the trick. The last pair flashed off into the dense undergrowth.

Fargo winced when he saw what they had done to Tom Johnson. The man's neck was ripped to shreds, a cheek was missing, and his lips had been torn off. As if that weren't grisly enough, his belly and thighs had been bitten into, the flesh peeled back like the skin of an orange.

The shovel was nearby, lying where the guard had dropped it. Propping the Henry against a tree, Fargo began to enlarge the small hole they had already made. Furtive rustling and the glint of wolfen eyes showed how determined the pack was not to give up their prize just yet.

A blur of gray arrowing through a crackling brush gave Fargo a split-second forewarning. In the blink of an eye he had the Colt out and up, and he fanned the trigger with the heel of his other hand. Fanning a gun tended to spray lead at random, but at close range it could be highly effective.

Three bullets caught the wolf in the center of its chest and lifted it off its paws. Tumbling in a whirl of hairy limbs and bushy tail, it rolled to a stop against an oak.

A howl went up from one of the others, perhaps its mate, and soon all the wolves were protesting to the heavens, the wavering chorus of their feral cries like an eerie dirge of the damned.

Fargo returned to his digging. A shallow grave was out of the question; the wolves would only dig Johnson up again. He had to dig down deep, a minimum of four feet. That would take some doing.

Fargo shoveled for the better part of an hour. It helped that the earth was so soft. Up in the Rockies a man could dig all night and half the day and hardly make a dent in the ground.

At last the hole was big enough. As Fargo stooped to slide the body in, footsteps crunched behind him. Whirling, he dropped his hand to the Colt but it was only Smithers, bearing a lantern. "What are you doing out here?"

"Mr. Carver sent me to check on you, sir. He said I was the only one you wouldn't shoot or pistol-whip." The butler hiked the lantern higher so he could see Johnson clearly. "Oh, my! I'm glad I ate a light supper."

"Grab his ankles," Fargo directed, wrapping his own hands around Johnson's wrists. "We'll lower him in together."

"Must I, sir?"

"Just don't look at him and you'll be fine," Fargo suggested.

"If you say so," Smithers said skeptically. Setting down the lantern, he said squeamishly, "I've never touched a dead person before."

"They don't bite."

Smithers rolled his eyes. "Try not to take this personally, sir, but has anyone ever mentioned that your sense of humor leaves a lot to be desired?" Taking a breath, he made bold to hold on to the corpse's feet.

"On the count of three," Fargo said, and counted down. They lifted in unison, Smithers staggering under the weight, and moved to the edge of the hole. "Try not to drop him," Fargo coaxed.

"The wonder will be that I don't fall in, myself," Smithers replied, his legs as wobbly as a drunken sailor's. He looked past Fargo and tensed. "I say! Some wolves are right behind you! I can see their eyes!"

"Are they standing there with their tongues hanging out?"

Smithers stared intently. "Yes, sir, as a matter of fact they are. Is that a sign they're about to devour us?"

"No, they're just curious. If they were going to attack, they'd crouch and bare their teeth." Which wasn't always true. Fargo just wanted to put the butler at ease.

"I wish I knew as much about animal nature as you do," Smithers said by way of praise.

"It's human nature you need to worry about," Fargo said. "Now let's get this over with." They carefully lowered the body. Then, squatting, Fargo leaned down to fold Johnson's arms across his chewed chest and closed both of the farmer's blank eyes.

"Just watching you do that has my stomach in knots," Smithers said. "I'm afraid I'd make a pitiful frontiersman."

"So? I'd make a rotten butler." Reclaiming the shovel, Fargo commenced filling in the grave.

Smithers picked up the lantern and gazed toward the clearing. "I can't take much longer or Mr. Carver will be mad. He's been doing his utmost to keep us separated."

"I've noticed." Fargo also noticed more wolves fading into the inky vale of night. Soon they would all be gone.

"He doesn't trust me," Smithers said. "Nor anyone else for that matter." Stepping closer, he spoke urgently. "I tried to let you know the other day that I had overheard a plot being hatched to eliminate you. I was walking by the quarters shared by Mr. Meachum and Mr. Banner when I distinctly heard Mr. Meachum say he liked Mr. Banner's idea a lot, that it would be the last thing you would expect."

"What else?" Fargo needed particulars.

"That's all I overheard, I'm sorry to say," Smithers answered. "I might have learned more but just then Mr. Carver came around the corner. I had to go on about my tasks."

The information had not been of much help, but Fargo thanked the butler anyway.

"Now, if you'll excuse me," Smithers said, leaving. "I don't want Mr. Carver to send his bully-boys after me."

As the lantern light receded into the trees, gloom shrouded the woodland. Fargo filled in the hole and tramped on the dirt, then went to the trouble of scouring the area for large fallen limbs and rocks with which to cover the mound. It was an added measure to keep scavengers from helping themselves to the remains.

It had taken so long that when Fargo wearily ambled into camp, almost everyone else had crawled back under their blankets and were sound asleep. The notable exceptions were Timmons and Dulcie.

Fargo didn't fail to note how the private secretary was dwelling on the blonde's charms. Timmons was startled when Fargo suddenly appeared beside the fire.

"Mr. Fargo! I had almost forgotten 'bout you. Is the deed done?"

Nodding, Fargo discarded the shovel, placed the

Henry on his bedding, and retrieved his coffee cup. The pot was still half full. Pouring some, he sank down with a sigh, the warmth of the fire a welcome treat for his sore muscles.

Dulcie wore a heavy robe wrapped around her shapely body. Her long golden tresses cascaded over it in rolling waves, hanging almost to her waist. She had lovely blue eyes and some of the whitest teeth Fargo had seen on any woman. Taking a sip of coffee from a china cup, she remarked, "I don't see how you could stay out there alone. I'd be too scared."

"You get used to it," Fargo said.

"I could live to be a thousand and never have your kind of courage," the dove said. "Why, when I was a little girl, the sight of a bumblebee drove me into a panic."

Fargo smiled. He liked how her lips had a natural delectable pout to them. And how her tiny nose curled at the tip. She looked much younger than she was, which Fargo guessed to be in her mid- to late twenties.

Timmons coughed and shifted. "Well, I suppose we should turn in, Miss Rose. It is rather late."

"You go ahead," Dulcie said without looking at him. "I'm not tired. I think I'll stay up a bit yet with Mr. Fargo, here."

"Oh." Timmons's expression was a lot like that of a man who had just been socked in the gut. "Are you sure? I mean, we have another long day in the saddle ahead of us tomorrow. We need plenty of rest."

"I'm a country gal," Dulcie said. "I can ride from dawn to dusk and it doesn't bother me a bit. Paula and Tricia are the ones you need to worry about. The only riding they've ever done is in bed."

Fargo chuckled, but Timmons flushed crimson and stiffly rose.

"Really, Miss Rose. That kind of talk isn't quite proper for mixed company. You must remember to behave like a lady."

The blonde glanced sharply at the mouse. "Go to bed, little man. I'm a grown woman, and I do as I damn well please. And no one tells me how to act. Ever. You remember that if you ever want to enjoy my company again."

Crestfallen, walking with his head bowed, Timmons retired. He gave Dulcie a last forlorn gaze, then lay with his back to the fire.

"Why is it," the dove said, speaking more to herself than to Fargo, "that some men can't let a woman be herself? Why do they make us out to be more than we are? We sweat and snore and pass gas just like men do."

"Some men like their women on pedestals," Fargo commented.

Dulcie's lips quirked upward. "How about you, big fella? How do you like your gals?"

"On their backs with their legs spread wide."

Laughter spilled from the dove like water bubbling over a waterfall. She laughed so loud, she had to clamp a hand to her mouth to keep from waking everyone up.

Timmons rose on an elbow to look at them, sadly shook his head, and sank back down, pulling his blanket up over his head.

When Dulcie finally controlled her mirth, she winked and said, "You're my kind of man, big fella. You don't put on airs."

Fargo was grateful for her company. Her light-hearted mood helped to dispel the glum frame of mind he had been in since Tom Johnson was slain. She, and women like her, were the reason he didn't live in the wilderness permanently. Females were a tonic for the spirit, as invigorating as any cure ever sold by patent medicine salesmen. "So you're a country girl?"

"Born and bred on a small farm in Ohio," Dulcie said. "I left when I was seventeen. Ran off with a no-account from the local tavern who promised me the world and gave me the gutter."

"You've been on your own ever since?"

"More or less. There have been other fellas but none ever worked out." Dulcie stared into the fire.

"It's hard for a gal to make ends meet nowadays, so I wound up being friendly for a living."

Her tone told Fargo that for all her talk about putting on airs and such, she didn't like what she was doing. "Ever wish you could go back home again?"

"I used to," Dulcie confessed, growing wistful. "But my pa would have tanned my hide until I bled. And Ma, well, it would crush her heart to learn what I've made of my life."

"Do something else, then. It's never too late to change."

"I've thought about it. Lord knows I have! Maybe once this is over I'll move somewhere folks don't know me and start over. Atlanta sounds real nice. I can sew pretty fair, so I figure on talking a seamstress into taking me in as her helper."

To the west a series of wavering howls rippled across the grassland. The wolves were still on the prowl.

Dulcie listened for a moment, then sidled closer to him by wriggling her bottom. "Landsakes, that makes my skin crawl," she said loudly, as if she were scared. Scanning the sleepers, she bent toward him and whispered, "There's something I've been meaning to say to you."

Fargo lowered his face to hers. Up close she was stunningly beautiful, and it was all he could do to keep from kissing her. "I haven't been hard to find," he joked.

"I need to be mighty careful. She'd stick her dagger into my ribs quick-like if she found out."

"Who?"

"Who else, dummy? Paula. I know what the two of you did. But I bet *you* don't know that Carver paid her extra to do it. She's his, lock, stock, and barrel."

"But Carver almost killed her," Fargo said.

"Sure he did. When she demanded more money to keep spying on you. That's what they were arguing about when he pushed her." Dulcie paused. "So tell me—how does it feel to be played for a jackass?"

10

Fort Kearney had quite a history.

It wasn't the first post to bear the name. Fifteen years before, Colonel Stephen Kearney of the 1st U.S. Dragoons had established a fort much further east, at the mouth of Table Creek. It was intended to protect travelers using the Oregon Trail from marauding Indians and outlaws. But the army had deemed the site too far removed from the trail to be effective, and had insisted that a new site be found.

First Lieutenant Daniel Woodbury of the Corps of Engineers was given the chore. He picked a spot on the south side of the Platte River, within spitting distance of the rutted track winding westward. The army was pleased. But the Pawnees weren't, since it was in the middle of their territory. So First Lieutenant Woodbury did something rare. He offered the Pawnees more for the parcel than it was really worth— two thousand dollars in trade goods, and not cheap trinkets, either. Woodbury demanded that they receive decent goods, and they did. Small wonder the Pawnees thought so highly of him. Small wonder, too, the majority of the Pawnees had been friendly to whites ever since.

It was a shame, Skye Fargo often reflected, that more white men weren't like Woodbury. Relations between the red man and the white would have been much better than they were.

The new post, called New Fort Kearney by most people, was well situated, unlike some other posts Fargo had seen. He never could understand why the army had a habit of building forts where there was no water, scant game, and little wood. New Fort Kearney had all three in abundance.

On this sunny morning, scores of wagons were at rest along the Platte, parked in the grass close to the fort's high log walls. Two or three wagon trains, Fargo estimated, stopping to rest and stock up before they pushed on into the unknown. Pilgrims bustled about like ants. He saw men fishing in the Platte, women gathered in sewing circles sharing gossip, and families picnicking. They were happy, content, confident. Only because they had no idea what was in store for them.

The palisade's main gate was wide open. Troopers were stationed on guard on both sides of the double doors. Soldiers also manned towers on the ramparts at the corners, keeping a watchful eye on everything.

The post was packed with people. Emigrants were everywhere, as were soldiers, settlers, frontiersmen, and Indians. Not just Pawnees, either. Some Arapaho and Cheyenne were present, as well as a few Otoes.

The hub of activity seemed to be the sutler's shop. Goods were flying out the door as fast as the clerks could fill orders. As soon as the wagon trains departed, things would quiet down, but until then, bedlam reined.

Fargo angled toward a hitch rail along the west wall. The smell of sweat and horses and dust was heavy in the air. He saw four untended lavish wagons parked at the far end of the parade ground and guessed who they belonged to.

Jace Carver drew rein next to the pinto, announcing, "I have business to attend to, Fargo. You're on your own until tomorrow morning. I always have breakfast at the mess with the officers, so we'll leave about eight."

"Fine by me," Fargo said.

Meachum and Banner rode up, followed by Paula. She smiled sweetly and Fargo touched a finger to his hat brim to acknowledge it.

After what Dulcie Rose had revealed the other

night, Fargo didn't trust the redhead any further than he could heave a bull buffalo. Dulcie had claimed that Paula only pretended to be friendly, that her whole purpose was to learn how he felt about Carver and what his plans were. Even that business on the riverboat about sneaking from her compartment and then hiding from Meachum and Banner had been staged to convince him she was sincere.

Fargo had balked at the claim, at first. He thought maybe Dulcie was the one trying to deceive him, that Carver had put her up to it to turn him against Paula. So the day after Dulcie told him, he had put Paula to the test.

They had stopped to rest the horses when the sun was directly overhead, and the women ambled to the river to cool themselves off. Carver was busy with Timmons, so Fargo had slipped around through the brush to the gravel bar on which the women were resting. When the redhead looked around, he beckoned.

"I'll be right back," Paula told her friends, and sashayed over. "It's been a while since we last talked, handsome."

"Don't blame me," Fargo had said.

"It's Carver," Paula replied. "He won't let me out of his sight. Hell, he won't let any of us stray off. If he could get away with it, I swear he'd brand us like cattle." She had hooked her satiny arm through his. "What did you want to see me about?"

Fargo had watched her face closely. The next few moments were crucial. "I heard Meachum and Banner talking," he fibbed to test her reaction. "According to them, the real reason Carver shoved you that night you fell over the side was because you wanted more money to spy on me."

Shock marred Paula's features. She recovered quickly, but for an instant, a fleeting instant, the terrible truth was plainly mirrored deep in her eyes. "Why, that's the silliest thing I've ever heard! You ought to know better."

Fargo had smiled and replied that yes, he should, and from that moment on, he did. Finally, he understood why Paula had tried so hard to persuade him it wasn't Carver's fault she had fallen overboard, and why she had virtually begged him not to tangle with Carver.

Fargo had added proof soon after their exchange. He saw the redhead say something to Carver, and not two minutes later Carver had a heated argument with his executive assistants, accusing them, no doubt, of carelessly allowing Fargo to eavesdrop. Little did Carver know.

Now it was Dulcie Rose who drew rein at the hitch rail. "So this is an army fort, huh? I've never been in one before."

"Allow me," Fargo said, stepping to her mare and holding up his arms to lower her down. "I'll show you around."

"What a gallant gentleman you are, kind sir," Dulcie teased. Slowly sliding from the saddle, she rubbed her slender hips and then her bulging bosom against his chest as if to entice him with a foretaste of her wonderful charms. "I'd like nothing better. But Carver ordered us women to meet him at the headquarters building as soon as we freshen up."

"Another time, then," Fargo said.

Dulcie cupped his chin and said in earnest, "I'll take that as a promise, and hold you to it." Puckering her lips, she blew a kiss at him, giggled, and hurried to catch up with her companions, her shapely bottom drawing stares from several onlookers.

Fargo made a circuit of the post. He saw troopers in the cavalry yard saddling their mounts to go on patrol. He watched the blacksmith heat a strip of metal in a forge. He listened as a couple of Arapahos haggled with a grizzled mountain man over a beaver hat of his they had taken a shine to. He grinned at the antics of children scampering all about.

About to pass the mess, Fargo stopped when several

soldiers filed out. One of them, an officer, drew up short.

"Skye Fargo, as I live and breathe! It's great to see you again." The officer pumped Fargo's hand. "Captain Travers. Assistant quartermaster. Maybe you remember me from Fort Defiance?"

The post Travers mentioned was down Arizona way, the first garrison established in the territory. Fargo had been there last about four years ago.

"We played cards one night with Major Harrison," Captain Travers said to jog his memory. "He cleaned you out, remember?"

"And bragged about it for a whole week," Fargo recollected.

"A whole month is more like it." Travers grinned. "What brings you to our neck of the plains? Colonel Ainsley never mentioned he was expecting you."

"I'm not here on army business. I'm with Jace Carver's party."

In a twinkling, the captain's cheerful attitude was gone with the breeze. "You're working for a snake in the grass like Carver? Why not just go around robbing people? It would amount to the same thing."

"I thought Carver and the army were on good terms," Fargo said. "He supplies all the forts out this way, I hear."

Captain Travers started to say something, then caught himself and surveyed the compound. "We should talk in private. Too many ears out here." He gestured at the mess. "How about if I treat you to the worst cup of coffee this side of the Big Muddy?"

Breakfast was long since over and the next meal wasn't for hours. Except for a few soldiers with rare free time on their hands, the spacious room was deserted. Travers chose a table as far away from everyone else as possible, and when he began to explain, he did so almost in a whisper.

"I've heard a lot of officers speak highly of you. They say you're the best scout alive, as dependable as the year is long. So it surprises me to no end to find you linked up with Jace Carver. Yes, he has an exclusive contract with the army. But between you, me, and the sally port, the army brass would just as soon he didn't."

Fargo didn't see how that was possible. "If they don't like him, why did they give him the contract?"

"Because he has powerful contacts in high places, is why. No less than the quartermaster general gave the order to deal exclusively with him." Captain Travers couldn't hide his disgust. "I suspect a few people in high places were bribed. A lot of money had to change hands for Carver to pull it off. But then, given how much he's stealing from the taxpayers, it was well worth it to him."

"Stealing?"

Travers grew so intensely angry he could barely contain himself. "Stealing, swindling, call it what you will. Carver overcharges on everything, Fargo. We're paying three to four times more for items than we did before he came along. The greedy pig is bleeding us dry." Fargo suddenly recalled Tom Johnson saying something similar right before he died, something about the settlers being sucked dry. "Why hasn't anyone complained?"

Travers sat back and snorted. "How long have you been scouting for the army? Officers who complain hurt their careers. You know that. Hell, I'd send off a letter to the secretary of war this minute if I thought it would do any damn good."

"Does Carver do the same thing to the settlers?"

"Does he ever!" Travers declared. "The man who owns the general store at Platteville was in here a couple of weeks ago. He told me that Carver makes them pay five to ten times as much for goods as the goods are worth, and he wanted me to do something about it. I felt sorry for him but my hands are tied. It's a civil matter."

The pieces of the puzzle were finally coming together. Fargo had a few questions yet, though.

"Carver told me he has exclusive contracts with all four of the new settlements."

"That he does. And the others are suffering, too, just like Platteville."

"Why did they sign with him when they could buy from any supplier?"

"That's just it. There *are* no other suppliers. Carver has crushed all his competitors, driving them out of business. The new settlements had no choice."

Fargo thought of another factor. New settlers wouldn't know what Jace Carver was really like. The coyote was probably all smiles and friendly as could be until he had the signature he needed on his contract. Then Carver tightened the screws.

It shed new light on Tom Johnson's sacrifice. Johnson had died to save his community from being financially strangled to death.

"I wish I could help them," Captain Travers was saying. "I really do. So does the post commander. But it's out of our jurisdiction."

"Is it true some Pawnees have been acting up?" Fargo changed the subject. Perhaps Carver had lied about that just as he lied about everything else.

"Heard about that, did you? It's a small band, seven or eight young warriors led by a troublemaker the whites call Slash Nose. They say his nose was nearly cut in half during a fight with the Sioux." Travers swirled the coffee in his cup. "We'd love to get our hands on him but the friendly Pawnees won't help. They think he's bad medicine."

"Has his band attacked any of the settlers?"

"He hasn't harmed anyone, if that's what you mean. If he did, we could take the field against him in force. He's more of a nuisance than anything. A peculiar sort of nuisance." The captain sat back. "Shortly after each new settlement was formed, Slash Nose showed up to harass them. He ran off some stock, destroyed some property. Then he left."

Fargo sensed Travers had more to say.

"The strange thing is, Slash Nose has never gone

back to bother them again. Just the one time at each place, for a few weeks or so, and that was it. Usually young hotheads like him won't rest until they've driven the whites out. Especially when they're fired up with whiskey."

Since it was illegal for anyone to sell liquor to Indians, Fargo asked, "Did he steal some?"

"Not that we know of. Yet the friendly Pawnees tell us Slash Nose can somehow get his hands on cases of it, whenever he wants."

"Maybe a whiskey peddler is in the area," Fargo suggested.

"And hasn't sold his rotgut to any of the other Pawnees or any other tribe?" Captain Travers shook his head. "That's not how whiskey peddlers operate. They don't make any money supplying their poison to just one warrior."

At the word "supply" a flash of insight filled Fargo. He remembered Jace Carver saying some Pawnees were demanding more tribute to cross their territory. Suppose whiskey was the tribute? And suppose it wasn't tribute at all, but payment for services rendered for harassing the new settlements? What did Carver stand to gain, Fargo asked himself, by having Slash Nose cause trouble?

Captain Travers unwittingly supplied the answer. "Slash Nose has all the settlers on edge. They're scared he'll go on the warpath, so they've stockpiled enough arms and ammunition to fight a war."

Inwardly, Fargo smiled. The last piece of the puzzle was now in place. "Arms and ammunition they bought from Jace Carver at inflated prices?"

"Who else would they get it from?" Travers said bitterly.

Fargo reached across the table and shook the surprised officer's hand. "I want to thank you, Captain. You've been of tremendous help to me. And I think I know how I can repay you."

Travers was confused. "I have? How? Repay me for what?"

"The less you know, the better." Fargo rose. "Let's just say that in a short while, the army's problem and the settlers's worries will be over." He hurried out, leaving the officer scratching his head. Fargo had an idea, and as risky as it was, if he was very careful, he could pull it off.

Fargo searched for any Pawnees about the fort, particularly young warriors. He saw several older ones, whole families, a few women, and then finally near the sutler's, a pair of young braves who had just traded for a new red blanket and were admiring it.

They glanced up when Fargo tapped the tallest one on the shoulder. His fingers flying fluidly, he asked in sign language, "Question? Speak white tongue?"

"Little bit," the tall Pawnee responded.

"I want you to do me a favor," Fargo said. "If you do, I'll buy you another blanket just like the one you have."

Furrows creased the tall warrior's bronzed brow. "What mean 'favor'?"

"You do something for me, I do something for you," Fargo said.

The pair consulted in the Pawnee tongue. Then, rather suspiciously, the tall one asked, "What want me do?"

"I want you to take a message to Slash Nose."

"Not know him," the warrior instantly replied.

"Maybe you don't," Fargo said, which he very much doubted. "But you can still get word to him if you want. Through a friend of a friend, maybe. What harm can it do? One little message?"

"What message?" The tall warrior was more suspicious than ever.

"I want Slash Nose to meet me at the red rock on the north side of the Platte in three sleeps," Fargo said. The red rock was a boulder the size of a log cabin, a landmark known to most Indians and frontiersmen. It was so close to the river that each year, more and more mud and debris collected around it.

Eventually, a flood would bury it entirely. "Tell Slash Nose it's about his whiskey. He'll understand."

"That all?"

"That's all you have to do," Fargo said. "Do you want another new blanket or not?" Blankets weren't cheap on the frontier. Quality ones sold for upward of ten dollars. "Do we have a deal?"

Once more the Pawnees huddled. Grunting, the tall one finally said, "You buy blanket, we do 'favor.'"

"Wait here."

Emigrants were crammed shoulder to shoulder in the sutler's. Voices buzzed like a swarm of bees. Last-minute purchases were being made, everything from flour to harnesses to axes. Women were fingering swatches of material and daydreaming of dresses they'd like to fashion. Men were examining guns, knives, and tools. Children gazed hungrily at glass jars full of hard candy. Three clerks were doing the best they could to keep up with demand.

Fargo wound through the throng to a shelf piled high with blankets. Since Indians had a special fondness for bright colors, the sutler stocked a lot of gaudy hues to suit their tastes. Fargo grabbed a red one and waded toward the counter, where customers were lined three deep.

At the rate things were going, Fargo figured it would take half an hour to make his purchase. He was worried the two Pawnees might not stick around that long. With so much at stake, he couldn't let that happen. So he pushed through to the front and pounded on the counter to get a clerk's attention.

"Well, I never!" an elderly matron declared.

"How unspeakably rude," chimed in someone else.

A slight, scrawny clerk flexed his authority, "I beg your pardon, sir, but you'll have to wait your turn like everyone else."

Fargo shoved the blanket at him. "How much?"

"Didn't you hear me? Our policy is first come, first served. Go back to the end of the line and be patient like everyone else."

"How much?" Fargo repeated, casually lowering his right hand to the Colt.

"Now, see here—" The skinny clerk glanced down at the revolver, then at Fargo, then at the revolver again. "Eighteen dollars."

That was twice as much as the blanket should cost, and Fargo knew who he had to thank for it. He paid anyway.

The Pawnees were right where he had left them, and when Fargo walked up, the shorter warrior snatched the red blanket as if afraid Fargo would change his mind. As they started to go, Fargo said, "You won't forget my message?"

"Red rock. Three sleeps. Whiskey," the tall one quoted. Off they went.

Pleased at how well it had gone, Fargo turned and took a single step. Ten feet away were Meachum and Banner. They had seen the whole thing.

"What was that all about?" Meachum quizzed, coming closer.

"It doesn't concern you," Fargo responded.

"Everything you do concerns us, mister," Banner said. "Mr. Carver wants us to keep a close eye on you until we reach Finlay's Bend."

"He has you spying on me?" Once again Carver had overstepped himself but Fargo wasn't going to make an issue of it, not when doing so might spoil the plan he had put into motion.

"Not spying, exactly," Meachum said with oily contempt.

"Think of us as your two new shadows," Banner said, rubbing salt into the affront. "Where you go, we go."

Fargo placed his hands on his hips. "Do you remember what happened the night Johnson was shot?"

Meachum refused to be cowed. "What are you going to do? Pistol-whip us in front of all these people? The commanding officer wouldn't like that much, would he?"

Shoving them aside, Fargo walked toward the mess.

In case his plan didn't work out as he hoped, he needed to take steps to make sure the women weren't harmed. Granted, Paula was in Carver's pocket, and granted, she had used him, but she didn't deserve to die because of it.

Captain Travers wasn't in the mess, though. Fargo went back out and surveyed the crowded parade ground. Trying to spot a single trooper was like looking for a blue-coated needle in an already blue haystack.

Instead, Fargo headed for the headquarter's building. He could always leave word for Travers to get hold of him before Carver's party departed the next morning. Halfway across he was reminded of the four wagons at the far end of the parade ground, and noticed the front end of the lead wagon poking from between the hospital and the guardhouse.

Veering toward them, Fargo looked behind him for sign of Meachum and Banner. In their bowler hats they should be easy to spot, but he couldn't find them. To throw them off the scent, he entered the hospital.

"May I help you?" asked an officer with a stethoscope around his neck. He was scribbling furiously in a notebook.

"Is there a back door?" Fargo asked.

"Why, yes. Go around that way." The officer pointed at a narrow corridor. "Is that all you need?"

"A lot of luck would help," Fargo said. Once around the corner, he jogged to the rear, noting three empty rooms as he passed. Slipping outside, he ran around the northeast corner.

The wagons were lined up in a row, tongue to gate, with canvas covering the merchandise piled in their beds. None of Carver's hired guns were standing watch. There was no need, not when no one in their right mind would try to steal something in broad daylight in the middle of a military post.

Fargo pried at the canvas covering the last wagon. It had been tied down, and in order to see underneath he had to unfasten several of the knots. Wooden crates were stacked high. Some were marked "Farm Tools," other "Dry Goods." Toward the front, against the seat, were two small crates with no markings at all.

Untying more knots, Fargo pushed the canvas back far enough to pull one of the small crates out. He set it down, glanced both ways, then drew the Arkansas toothpick and pried at the thin slats. Nails gave way with tiny squeaks. Pulling and tugging, he loosened one enough to see the bottles inside.

Moving quickly, Fargo slid the second small crate out, stacked it on top of the first, then secured the canvas so no one would suspect it had been tampered with. Lifting both, he carried them to the hospital's rear door and went in.

None of the staff were anywhere in sight. Hastening to the nearest empty room, Fargo shoved the two crates under a bed. Odds were, no one would discover them for quite some time.

Fargo then walked to the front entrance. The officer with the stethoscope was gone but a comely nurse smiled at him.

"Have a nice day, sir."

"It's shaping up that way," Fargo said. Everything depended on whether Carver or his men realized the crates were missing. Pushing the door open, he strode into the sunlight. Meachum and Banner were still nowhere around.

Fargo walked toward the headquarters building. A flag was flapping atop a pole out in front. Fargo's attention was suddenly drawn to a commotion that had broken out to his left. Men, women, and children were scurrying every which way, their panic caused by a man in a frock coat with a rifle wedged to his shoulder.

It was Guzman.

11

For several seconds Skye Fargo was rooted by surprise. He couldn't quite accept the evidence of his own eyes. A small voice in his head insisted it was impossible, that Guzman couldn't possibly be here, being that they were hundreds of miles away from Kansas City.

Yet there was no denying that it certainly looked like Guzman, and no denying that the man's features were twisted in the same mask of fury Guzman wore at the gambling hall and again during their fight at Molly's. Nor would it do to ignore the threat posed by the business end of Guzman's leveled rifle.

Fargo flung himself to the ground, the blast ringing in his ears as a leaden hornet nipped his hat. He rolled to the left a fraction before another slug spewed dirt and dust within an inch of his head.

Women and children screamed, men yelled, the racket they made drowned out by the boom of Guzman's next shot, which clipped Fargo's left sleeve. Pushing up from his prone position, Fargo palmed the Colt.

A family of emigrants had blundered into Guzman's line of fire and he was shifting to get clear of them.

They fired simultaneously, and Fargo swore he felt a tiny breeze fan his cheek. Guzman staggered, grit his teeth, then raised his rifle to try again as Fargo thumbed off a second shot, then a third.

Thunder echoed off the high palisade walls.

Guzman was on his knees now, but far from finished. Stooped over, beads of sweat dotting his brow, he was painfully raising his Spencer.

Fargo took precise aim. A slug to the head would end it. But suddenly steely arms caught hold of his own, and he found himself in the grip of two beefy troopers intent on stopping the gunfight.

"There'll be no more shooting, mister!" a private declared.

"This is a military post!" the other said, as if that had any bearing on the situation.

Fargo hadn't taken his eyes off Guzman.

The gambler had pressed his cheek to the rifle stock. Blood was trickling from his mouth and large scarlet circles had formed on his chest, yet his mouth curled in a vicious grin. Thanks to the troopers, Fargo was a perfect target.

More soldiers were rushing toward the scene. None, though, were anywhere near the gambler. None could stop him from firing.

Fargo tried to shake free but the troopers holding him were big, brawny men. Iron fingers had him by the wrist, so he couldn't point the Colt. He saw Guzman steady himself and Fargo braced for the searing impact of the slug. At the loud crack, Fargo involuntarily flinched.

There was no pain, no hard blow, nothing. No gunsmoke wreathed the end of the gambler's rifle.

Guzman appeared as puzzled as Fargo. His arms sagged and he glanced down at himself, at a new stain in the center of his shirt. Groaning, he pitched onto his face, his back arched like a bow, his arms limp at his sides.

Captain Travers stepped into view, his revolver extended, wisps of smoke rising from the muzzle. Carefully approaching Guzman, he kicked the rifle from the gambler's hands, then turned around. "Let go of him," he ordered the troopers.

The soldiers obeyed, but they both dropped their hands to their own revolvers and regarded Fargo as they would a cornered cougar.

"What was this all about?" Captain Travers asked.

Briefly, Fargo told about his run-in with the gambler, ending with, "I thought I'd seen the last of him. I don't know how he got here."

By then they were surrounded by soldiers and civilians, all craning to see Guzman. At a crisp command from a newcomer, they parted, allowing an older officer wearing the insignia of a full colonel to make his way through. At his heels were Jace Carver, Meachum, and Banner, and the three doves.

"Colonel Ainsley, allow me to introduce Skye Fargo," Captain Travers said, snapping to attention.

"I've heard of you," the commanding officer said, shaking. To a nearby trooper, he barked, "Sergeant! Fetch Lieutenant Layton and a stretcher from the hospital! On the double!"

"Yes, sir!"

Fargo had to explain his connection to the gambler a second time for the benefit of Ainsley, who squatted and rolled Guzman over.

The gambler was still alive, his breathing shallow, his face as pale as a sheet. But his eyes were pools of roiling hatred. "Almost had you, bastard," he spat, pink froth rimming his lips.

Colonel Ainsley put a hand on his shoulder. "Are you insane, Mr. Guzman? To discharge a firearm among all these people? What were you thinking?"

"I want him dead," Guzman weakly answered. "Came all this way . . . followed him from Kansas City . . . riverboat . . . up the trail . . ." His eyelids fluttered and he couldn't go on.

"Merely to exact revenge?" Colonel Ainsley said in disbelief. "Over a trifle like being caught cheating?"

"It's not a trifle to me!" Guzman found the energy to reply. "He shamed me! Made me out to be a fool! I'll make worm food of him if it's the last—"

"You're killing days are over," Colonel Ainsley broke in. "If you live, you'll be brought up on charges and spend the next five to ten years behind bars."

The gambler glared at Fargo. "This isn't over. I'll get you. No matter how long it takes. Whatever I have to do. I'll get you."

Colonel Ainsley made a clucking sound. "You *are* insane. I'll send for the chaplain in case you want to cleanse your soul before you go to meet your Maker."

Guzman tried to spit on the officer. "I don't want a damn minister! I'm not going to die!" Again he glared at Fargo. "I should have waited. But when I saw you, I couldn't help myself. I—" Just like that, he passed out.

Sighing, the colonel stood. "You meet all kinds in this world."

Lieutenant Layton arrived with two stretcher bearers. It turned out Layton was the officer with the stethoscope Fargo had spoken to earlier. He hastily examined Guzman, then announced, "I need to operate right way. There's a slim chance I can save him if I act fast."

"Get to it then," Colonel Ainsley said.

After the gambler was carted off and the crowd was ordered to disperse, Colonel Ainsley turned to Fargo. "We're having a special meal this evening in honor of Mr. Carver's visit. I would be greatly honored if you would attend."

Fargo was going to decline. He wanted little to do with Carver. But when he saw the flicker of annoyance Carver was unable to hide, and the sly grin Dulcie gave him, he changed his mind. "Be glad to."

The gunfight was on everyone's lips. For the rest of the day, wherever Fargo went on the post, people pointed or whispered behind his back. Mothers clutched their children and men gave him a wide berth.

At three that afternoon, Fargo visited Captain Travers in Travers's office and outlined his plan.

Afterward, the captain sat in thoughtful silence awhile, saying at last, "You realize the enormous risk you're taking, don't you? Not only with your life, but those of the women as well?"

"That's why I'm counting on you to be there when you're needed."

"I should refuse. I should walk right out and report

this to the colonel. But, technically, you're not doing anything illegal. And, God help me, Carver has it coming. I just pray it doesn't blow up in your face."

"That makes two of us."

At seven o'clock Fargo showed up at the mess. The enlisted men had already eaten and gone. Two long tables had been placed end to end at the head of the room, and seated around it were the fort's officers and Jace Carver's party. Colonel Ainsley had saved a seat between Captain Travers and himself, and directly across from Dulcie Rose.

"I'm glad you could make it," the colonel said warmly.

Jace Carver wasn't happy at all, although he tried hard not to show it. "Fargo," he said simply, the coldness in his gaze putting the lie to the slight smile he plastered on his face.

A door along the north wall swung open and out hustled Smithers bearing a silver tray. "Ladies and gentlemen," he announced grandly, "supper is served." He brought the tray over. "The appetizer will be tomato and onion soup. The main course will consist of beef au gratin, plus salad and vegetables. Dessert will be chocolate pudding. Quite delicious, if I do say so, myself."

Colonel Ainsley nudged Carver. "This cook of yours is sensational. Do you eat like this every night?"

"Cook?" Jace Carver cackled, "I hire only *chefs* to work at my estates. Smithers, here, is neither. He's my butler. Oh, he's a fair hand with a spoon and spatula, which is why I bring him along on these treks. But my Parisian chef puts him to shame."

They launched into a long talk about food, with Carver going on and on about the differences between European and American cuisine.

Fargo couldn't have been more bored if he tried. He downed his soup and had just started in on the beef when he felt something brush his ankle. Thinking his legs must be stretched out too far and that the blonde had accidentally bumped him, he pulled his feet back toward his chair. Yet a moment later it happened again.

Dulcie was poking at her salad and hadn't seemed to notice.

Forking more beef into his mouth, Fargo took a couple of bites—and felt the contact again. This time Dulcie slowly rubbed her foot up and down his shin. And the whole while, she sat there eating as calmly as could be. No one would suspect what she as doing.

Why? Fargo reflected. Was she being playful? Or was it a sign she was interested in him? To find out, he rubbed his leg against hers, sliding his foot as high as her knee.

Dulcie never showed the least little reaction.

Fargo felt her toes rising higher. They glided along his inner thigh to within a few inches of his manhood, which was as far as she could extend her foot. His legs, though, were a lot longer, as she learned when he rubbed the side of his boot up hers.

The gleam in Dulcie's beautiful blue eyes when she glanced at him hinted more was in store. But how that could be, Fargo wondered, when Carver had the women on such a short leash, was beyond him.

Shortly after eight someone else showed up. Lieutenant Layton sank into an empty chair, saying, "My apologies, sir, for being so late. The operation took much longer than I anticipated."

"What's the prognosis?" Colonel Ainsley asked.

"Guzman will recover," Layton reported. "I dug four slugs out of him, including one that missed his heart by a whisker, and he's lost a lot of blood. But given enough time, he'll mend and be fit to stand trial."

"Excellent," the colonel said. "I'd imagine you're glad to hear it, too, Mr. Fargo?"

Fargo wasn't. So long as Guzman was alive, he'd try to make good on his threats. "You'll keep him under guard?"

"Oh, most assuredly. And once he's on the mend,

he'll be transferred from the hospital ward to the stockade."

An hour later the meal ended. Colonel Ainsley invited Jace Carver and several senior officers to his quarters for cigars and brandy. He invited Fargo, too, but Fargo begged off, saying he was tired.

Meachum and Banner escorted the ladies off. Timmons was the only one left at the table when Fargo rose and ambled out into the crisp night air.

"Need a place to sleep?" Captain Travers was adjusting his jacket. "I have a cot you're welcome to use."

"No thanks," Fargo responded. "I've staked out a pile of straw at the stable." He'd visited the corporal on stable duty earlier and slipped him a dollar for the privilege.

"Suit yourself." Travers said. "But if you ask me, I could find more comfortable lodgings."

"At least Carver won't try anything here," Fargo predicted.

"I hope you're right." The captain headed across the compound.

Fort Kearney seemed unnaturally quiet after the daytime din. All the emigrants and Indians were gone, and most of the soldiers were in their barracks. The parade ground was virtually deserted.

Fargo hooked his thumbs in his gunbelt and slanted toward the stable. He was almost there when the patter of running feet brought him around in a crouch, his right hand stabbing for the Colt. When he saw who it was, he didn't know whether to be glad or worried. "What in blazes are you doing here?"

"Aren't you the romantic cuss!" Dulcie said, snickering. Her full figure and golden tresses were concealed by a flowing dark blue velvet cape with a hood. "And after all the trouble I went to climbing out the back window!" Her snicker became a laugh, which she stifled by covering her mouth.

"Won't your friends notice you're missing?" Fargo asked.

"It's not very likely," Dulcie said. "We're staying in a cabin reserved for guests of the colonel's, and we each have our own little bedroom. I told Paula and Tricia I wasn't feeling well and needed to turn in."

"I don't want you to get into trouble."

"Then we'd shouldn't dawdle." Dulcie clasped his hand. "Where can we be alone?"

The only place Fargo could think of was the stable. At that time of night all the horses had been bedded down and the stableman, a corporal, was off playing cards and drinking with his buddies.

Dulcie cocked her head. "Are you serious? In a hayloft? Why, I haven't done that since I was sixteen."

Fargo tried to come up with another idea, but other than a moonlit stroll by the river, which wasn't entirely safe, he was at a loss.

"Let's do it!" Dulcie abruptly exclaimed, pressing his hand to her bosom. "It'll be fun!"

Luckily, they encountered no one else. Fargo saw guards patrolling the parapet, and two more smoking cigarettes out by the sally port. One of the stable's wide double doors was cracked open, and ushering her inside, he closed and barred them both.

"What if someone wants to bring in their mount?" Dulcie said.

"They can knock."

Tittering, Dulcie yanked on his arm, leading him toward the ladder to the loft. "Last one up has to undress first."

Fargo dug in his heels, motioned toward the rear, and steered her toward a huge pile of straw next to the tack room. It was further from the entry and shrouded by shadow. "Now what was it you had in mind, minx?"

For an answer, Dulcie grabbed at his crotch with one hand while unhitching his buckle with the other. "Paula bragged about how good you are, and I want to find out for myself." Her hood fell down around her shoulders, her lustrous blond hair spilling almost to her narrow waist.

Fargo entwined his fingers in it, then stiffened as her hand slipped inside his buckskin pants and her palm wrapped around his hardening pole.

"Oh, yes," Dulcie gloated. "Paula wasn't exaggerating. You really *are* a stallion, aren't you?"

Fargo locked his lips to hers. Her mouth parted and her delicious tongue sought his, her fingers tracing delicate patterns lower down. When she cupped him, his manhood bulged.

"Oh my, oh my, oh my," Dulcie panted. "I've hit the mother lode."

Fargo kissed her again. Raising his hands to her breasts, he squeezed them through her dress, which caused her to grind her hips against him and utter a long moan.

"Keep that up and there's no telling what will happen," Dulcie purred.

Fargo's left hand strayed to her firm, rounded bottom, which he massaged while lowering her onto her back on the straw. It gave way under them, molding to the contours of their bodies. While he licked her neck and sucked on her earlobe, her hand swirled around and around his member, stoking his inner fire. She knew just where to touch driving him wild with desire.

Unfastening the buttons at the top of her dress, Fargo gained access to her underthings, which he parted to reveal her intoxicating charms. When her glorious globes spilled out, he greedily clamped his mouth on to a nipple. Her breasts were as round as grapefruits and as soft as pillows.

"Ahhhh. I like that," the blonde declared.

So did Fargo. He took his sweet time, massaging and caressing, kissing and sucking, until she wriggled under him in anxious anticipation.

Dulcie's hand continued to stroke his manhood. Every so often she would gently fold her fingers over the tip and make a pumping motion that came close to causing an eruption.

As much as Fargo was enjoying their lovemaking,

he couldn't let himself fully relax. He constantly listened for unusual sounds or the tread of footsteps. Once, he thought he heard the clomp of hooves and was about to rise when he realized it was the pounding of his own racing pulse.

For her part, Dulcie devoured him with abandon. Her hot mouth lavished fiery kisses galore as her other hand roamed everywhere; through his hair, across his broad shoulders, down to his backside, which she tweaked and rubbed, then up to his inner thigh. Soon her legs parted and her ankles hooked around him, pulling him closer.

"I'm ready for you, big man."

Fargo wasn't. He knew he should hurry in order to get her back to the guest cabin that much sooner, but a few more minutes shouldn't do any harm. His hand hiked at the folds of her dress, which rustled as he raised the hem up to her hips. Her legs were superb, so smooth that running his hand over them was like caressing marble.

Dulcie gasped when his finger brushed her moist slit. "Come on Fargo, play with me. I'm all yours!"

Not quite yet, Fargo thought, parting her nether lips. She eagerly thrust against him, groaning when he inserted his finger as far as it would go. Her thighs closed on his hand. Soon their mouths joined, Fargo sucking on her sweet tongue as he would on sugary caramel.

Dulcie was panting, little mews issuing from her throat. Her eyes burned with raw passion, and her body was hot to the touch. Letting go of his pole, she placed both hands on his back. "I want it now," she insisted.

Fargo began to stroke her with his finger. He was content to indulge in foreplay a little while longer. But suddenly she pushed at his arm, arched her spine, and impaled herself on his manhood, all in a quick, fluid motion. He felt her wet inner walls wrap around him, sheathing him to the hilt.

A tiny smile curled her full lips. "When I say now, I mean now."

For a few moments they were still, savoring the exquisite sensation. Then Dulcie commenced to lever her bottom upward, nearly lifting him out of the straw. Fargo propped his hands on either side and rocked on his knees, matching his rhythm to hers.

"Yes! Yes! Harder! Faster!"

Fargo obliged.

Dulcie's mouth found his, her nails clawing into his back, and had it not been for his buckskin shirt she would have drawn blood. She drove herself against him with passionate zest, her need even greater than his.

The feel of her rippling inner walls was almost enough to send Fargo over the edge. His explosion built to maddening heights, but he held off through sheer force of will. It was almost as if it had become a contest. She was doing her utmost to make him lose control, and he was doing all he could to prolong their coupling as long as possible.

Dulcie licked his ear, his throat. She entwined her fingers in his hair. Her hips slammed into him with rising vigor, as if they were a battering ram. "Yes! Ahhhhh! I'm there! I'm there!"

Although he sought to stave off his own release, it was impossible. Hers triggered his. He gushed like a geyser, driving up into her again and again. Their bed of straw and the wall behind them blurred, and all he could hear was the mutual husking of their heavy breaths and the slapping of their bodies.

Gradually, they rocked to a stop, Fargo lying on top of her, his nose in her long blond hair, inhaling her flowery scent. Her lips were close to his neck, and she pecked him lightly.

"You're really something baby. We should do this again when we have a lot more time on our hands."

"Just say when," Fargo said. Reluctantly, he fought off the lethargy that always followed, and willed himself to sit up. "We'd better get you back."

Dulcie frowned. "I know. Damn Carver all to hell."

Fargo helped her up and brushed straw from her clothes as she put herself together. They walked down the center aisle, Dulcie hanging on his arm and grinning like a cat that just ate a canary.

"So tell me, handsome. Which one of us did you like best? Paula or me?"

Fargo hesitated. Only an idiot would answer such a question. "That's like trying to pick between white wine and red," he tactfully replied. Not that he was much of a wine drinker.

"Clever." Dulcie grinned knowingly. "But that's all right. Don't make up your mind yet, not until you and I have a whole night to ourselves. Then I'll show you which one of us is better."

Removing the heavy bar, Fargo cracked open the right-hand door and scanned the parade grounds. Other than a trooper or two, the coast seemed clear. "Stay close to me," he cautioned, taking her hand.

"I wouldn't have it any other way."

Rather than cross all that open space, Fargo bore to the left, staying near the buildings where they were less likely to be spotted. "Where's the cabin you were assigned?" he asked.

Dulcie took the lead. It was one of several situated near the northwest corner of the post. Lights blazed in the front room, and through a sheer curtain Fargo glimpsed Paula and Tricia playing a game of dice. Dulcie guided him around to the rear and halted beside a darkened window. "This is my room," she whispered. Embracing him, she bestowed a lingering kiss, then smiled, quietly slid the window up, and vaulted in over the sill.

Fargo waited until she turned the latch before he crept to the front corner. Satisfied no one was nearby, he started toward the stable. He was halfway to the next cabin when, without warning, three figures hove out of the darkness. Dashing into inky shadow, he flattened against the log wall before they could spot him.

"—doesn't fool me for a second," a familiar voice growled. "Colonel Ainsley doesn't like me one bit. He only tolerates me because he has to."

Fargo peered out.

Jace Carver and his executive assistants came to the cabin, pausing at the door. "I advise you to get plenty of rest, gentlemen. Tomorrow we begin the last leg of our trip and we'll need our wits about us."

"Are we still going to take care of the Trailsman after we reach Finlay's Bend?" Meachum asked.

"That you will. But then, not until we get to Finlay, no matter how obnoxious he becomes. I'm counting on his vaunted skill to help us avoid Slash Nose. When that stinking heathen sees I can slip right by him, he'll settle for the amount we agreed on." Carver opened the door. "Ironic, isn't it? I'm using one nuisance to get the better of another."

"No one can outfox you, sir," Banner fawned.

Jace Carver beamed. "Truer words were never spoken."

=== 12 ===

On the third morning after the supply train left Fort Kearney, Skye Fargo told Jace Carver that he had found Indian sign in the mud along the Platte, and he wanted to make a sweep of the surrounding countryside.

"Do whatever is necessary," Carver directed. "I want to avoid hostiles at all costs."

Fargo rode on ahead, bringing the pinto to a trot once he was out of sight of the wagons. By his reckoning he was just ten miles from Red Rock, and he wanted to be there by noon. He could only hope Slash Nose showed up; everything depended on it.

The renegade was bound to have heard about Carver's arrival at the fort from other Pawnees. Curiosity, if nothing else, should bring him to the meeting place.

So far Fargo had seen no indication that anyone had noticed the missing crates. He doubted they would, since Carver had no intention of turning them over to Slash Nose except as a last resort.

The morning was warm and muggy. Birds chirped and flitted in the trees, while a large turtle sunned itself on a log out in the river. Far to the southwest, the squat shapes of a herd of grazing buffalo were silhouetted against the sky.

Red Rock, situated as it was along a stretch of the Platte where few trees grew, was visible from a quarter mile off. Fargo crossed to the north side, shucked the Henry from its scabbard, and levered a round into the chamber. Resting the rifle across his saddle, he approached at a walk.

No one appeared to be there but that didn't mean a thing. The Pawnees would lie low until they were sure it wasn't a trap.

Twenty yards out, Fargo drew rein. "Slash Nose!" he shouted, hoping that the renegade spoke at least a smattering of English. "I'm the man who sent for you. We need to palaver."

From out of the tall grass came a guttural command. "Drop yours guns, white-skin."

"No."

"You don't, maybe we kill you and take them, eh?"

"Kill me and you won't hear what I have to say," Fargo replied, refusing to back down. "That would be a mistake. Or don't you care Jace Carver intends to cheat you?"

Whispering ensued, and a stocky warrior soon rose, holding a Sharps. His attire consisted of a beaded sash, a breechcloth, and thigh-high fringed moccasins. Silver bands adorned both muscular arms. But the most distinguishing feature was his horribly disfigured nose. It was split across the middle where a blade once cut deep, leaving a twisted gash.

Other Pawnees stood, eight of them, most armed with bows. One carried a war club studded with spikes.

Cradling the Sharps, Slash Nose cautiously came closer. "Who are you, white man? Why do you tell me this?"

"Who I am isn't important," Fargo responded. "All you need to know is that I know about your deal with Carver. How he agreed to give you firewater if you caused trouble for the settlers."

"One case of whiskey each time his wagons visit the settlements," Slash Nose confirmed. "Carver said it is our secret."

"Jace Carver speaks with two tongues," Fargo declared. "He promises one thing and does another."

"You are his enemy?" Slash Nose asked.

"I am," Fargo admitted. To do otherwise would make the Pawnee suspicious of his motives.

"My ears are open to your words."

Fargo leaned on his saddle horn. "The last time the wagons came through, you told the drivers to tell Carver you wanted more whiskey from now on, didn't you?"

Slash Nose held up two fingers. "Two cases of whiskey, yes."

"It made Carver mad," Fargo said.

"Why? Carver has much money. More than all the blades of grass on the prairie, he told me."

"He's richer than most, that's for sure."

"Then why is he mad?" Slash Nose was sincerely confused. "One more case is not much to ask of someone who can buy so many."

"Carver is stingy with his money. He loves it above all else."

"This I have seen."

"Then you shouldn't be surprised to learn he's decided to make wolf meat of you rather than give you the extra firewater." Fargo saw some of the other warriors glance at one another. Evidently their leader wasn't the only one who had picked up some of the white man's tongue.

Slash Nose's jaw muscles twitched. "Carver would kill me for so little?"

"To him it's the principle of the thing," Fargo said. "No one tells him what to do. So he hired me to make sure he doesn't run into you. He'd rather slip in and out without you knowing. Show you that you have no power over him."

"Stay where you are."

Slash Nose backed away from the Ovaro, then gestured. His fellow Pawnees ringed him and a heated exchange took place. When it was over, he came forward. "Why do you tell me these things?"

"I told you. Carver is my enemy."

"There is more." Slash Nose posed it as a fact, not a question.

"I have no quarrel with the Pawnees. If blood is to be spilled, I want no part of it." Fargo had saved the best for last. "And Carver has women and a couple of others with him, people I don't want harmed should Carver and you tangle."

"So that is your reason." Slash Nose grunted. "What proof can you give that your words are true?"

"Carver is the proof. When the sun is there—" Fargo pointed at a spot in the sky equivalent to the middle of the afternoon—"the supply wagons will stop near the black tree east of here." He was referring to an old oak charred by lightning. "Do you know where it is?"

"I know this whole country, white-skin."

"Then come see if Carver has your whiskey. If I'm lying, he'll hand it over. If I'm telling the truth . . ." Fargo shrugged. "Do what you have to. All I ask is that you let me take the women and one or two others out of there before you start anything."

"If you have spoken with a straight tongue, I will do as you want," Slash Nose pledged.

Fargo went to rein around. "One last thing. Carver has many men with him, many rifles. Enough to gun all of you down before any of you nock an arrow."

"We are not easy to kill," Slash Nose said.

Nodding, Fargo tapped his spurs against the stallion. A tall Pawnee began to lift a bow but stopped at a word from their leader. Unwilling to tempt fate, Fargo kept his eyes on them until he was well out of arrow range. Then he trotted to the ford, returned to the south side of the Platte, and galloped off.

Carver had made better time than Fargo expected. The supply train was only a mile east of the black tree, with four guards riding point, six more at the rear. The rest were on the wagons.

Jace Carver cantered to meet him. "About time you got back," he snapped. "Did you find fresh sign?"

"Yes." Fargo saw that the women were situated between the first and second wagons. Dulcie, ever the tease, grinned and winked.

"Well?" Carver said impatiently. "Are they hostiles?"

"I can't tell from the tracks," Fargo said. Although, on occasion, he could. Hostiles were much more likely to use shod horses stolen from whites.

Carver swore. "Some help you are! I want to avoid a confrontation, remember? It's why I brought you along."

"The only way to do that is to spot them before they spot us," Fargo said. "We'll stop up ahead and I'll make another scout."

"Don't disappoint me, Trailsman," Carver said sternly. "I don't tolerate failures."

Fargo rode down the line to where Smithers was riding as stiff-backed as an ironing board. Wheeling in alongside him, Fargo said, "Nice day for a bloodbath."

"Sir?" The butler was at a total loss.

"We'll be resting the animals in a while. When we do, keep your eyes on me and be ready to do exactly as I tell you."

Some of the starch went out of Smithers's spine. "We're in for a bit of trouble, I take it?"

"More than a bit," Fargo said. "But keep it under your hat." He glanced back at where Carver's private secretary was plodding miserably along. He'd thought of warning Timmons, too, but he wasn't entirely convinced Timmons would keep quiet. "Stay close to him when the time comes, will you?"

"Certainly, sir."

Fargo spurred the pinto to the women. "Afternoon, ladies," he greeted them. "You might like to know we'll be stopping shortly."

"Good," Paula said. "My bottom is so sore from all this infernal riding, I can barely sit at night."

"Poor baby," Dulcie said in mock sympathy. "My bottom is just fine." She leered at Fargo. "You can examine it for yourself any time your little heart desires, handsome."

Unwittingly, the blonde had given Fargo the excuse he needed to lean toward her and whisper in her ear as if he were making a lewd comment. "Pretend I just told you something naughty, and giggle."

Dulcie was as sharp as she was beautiful. She giggled lustily.

"When we stop, keep your eyes on me," Fargo whispered. "Your life may depend on it."

"Will do, big man," Dulcie responded. "And I do mean *big*."

Paula and Tricia smiled at their antics, not suspecting a thing as Fargo returned to the front of the train.

Jace Carver, however, wasn't amused in the slightest. "What were you talking to the women about?"

"How to grow turnips," Fargo said, and moved on past the four guards until he was a hundred yards in front of the column. He had done what he could to warn those he wanted to spare from harm. Now he had to wait for the chain of events he had set in motion to unfold, and hope that everything worked out the way he wanted.

The trail wound along the meandering Platte, never straying from the river's edge. Many grooves had been worn into the soil by the passage of countless wagon wheels, and in some spots they were so deep, it almost looked as if a plow were to blame.

The black tree, unlike Red Rock, couldn't be seen from a long way off. It was in dense woodland, its uppermost branches gone, blasted to bits by the bolt out of the blue that had set the tree ablaze. Rain had smothered the fire before the trunk could be consumed, leaving a blackened husk.

Fargo had picked the spot for a reason. For most of its winding length the Platte's shoreline was as flat as the surrounding plain. But at the point where it flowed past the black tree, erosion had carved a steep bank over six feet high and thirty feet long. It would make an excellent shelter from stray bullets.

Reining up in the oak's shadow, Fargo scoured the vegetation for sign of the Pawnees. If they were there, they were well hidden. Fargo didn't dismount until the wagons arrived. Then, yanking the Henry out, he moved the stallion close to the bank and looped the reins in a bush.

Carver, Meachum, and Banner were sharing swigs from a silver flask. "How long do you expect us to wait here while you're on your scout?" Carver asked. "I don't like needless delays. We can cover another five miles before nightfall if we push on."

Fargo wasn't going anywhere if he could help it. "I'll leave as soon as I've watered my horse," he stalled. He saw Smithers and Dulcie both watching him closely.

"Then get to it," Carver commanded. "Time is wasting while you stand there like a bump on a log."

Fargo turned. All the mounted guards had climbed down and were resting or talking, and only a few were still up on the wagons. If Slash Nose intended to make an appearance, it was the ideal moment.

Slowly walking toward the Ovaro, Fargo scanned the undergrowth without being obvious. He was the first to see three riders emerge although he didn't let on that he had until Meachum hollered.

"Mr. Carver! Indians!"

Slash Nose and his two companions drew rein fifteen yards out. They sat as impassive as stones although excited guards were training Spencers on them.

Jace Carver glowered at Fargo like a mad bull about to charge, his expression saying more than words ever could. Then he faced the Pawnees, smiling as slick as ever. "Slash Nose, my friend! How good to see you again."

The renegade had a sense of humor. "If it is so good, white-skin, how is it you did not send word you were here?"

"You didn't know?" Carver acted shocked. "I asked a friendly Pawnee at the fort to tell you, but I guess he couldn't find you." Carver beckoned. "Climb down and sit awhile."

Slash Nose did no such thing. "I want the whiskey."

"Of course. But can't we talk awhile before we get

down to business? Never forget, you're always welcome in my camp."

"Am I?" Slash Nose nodded at the guards.

"Lower those guns, men!" Carver bawled. "I want our visitors to feel right at home." He looked toward the trees. "How many warriors are with you? Just the two?"

"I brought more," Slash Nose replied. "Many more."

"Have them show themselves," Carver said. "They have nothing to fear from me."

"They stay where they are."

Fargo could tell Jace Carver didn't like the situation one bit. Carver sensed something was wrong but he wasn't worried. Not yet, anyway.

"I am waiting," Slash Nose said.

"What's gotten into you?" Carver wanted to know. "I thought we had an agreement."

"I hear maybe you do not want to honor it. I heard maybe you want to cheat me."

Bewilderment delayed Carver's response. "Where did you hear such a thing? I made you a promise and I intend to keep it."

"Did your drivers tell you I want more whiskey?"

"One more case each trip, yes," Carver said. "And I brought two this time, exactly as you wanted."

"Show me," Slash Nose commanded.

Fargo wanted to signal Dulcie and Smithers but they were both gazing at Carver and the Pawnees.

It was as plain as the terrible scar on Slash Nose's face that Jace Carver resented being told what to do, especially by a lowly "heathen." When it came to others, Carver was a cheapskate through and through, and it was this, as much as his arrogance and bigotry, that was about to prove his undoing. He had brought it on himself by refusing to give in to the brave's demand for one measly extra case of cheap rotgut.

"The whiskey is in the last wagon," Carver informed Slash Nose. "Follow me and I'll show you."

151

Pivoting, he hurried toward it, with Meachum and Banner tagging along like a pair of trained dogs.

Slash Nose and his friends angled their mounts to the left, refusing to venture any closer to the guards. Slash Nose completely ignored Fargo as they went by.

For his part, Fargo was still trying to get the attention of the blonde and the butler. Aware of furtive movement in the woods, he sidled toward the women.

Jace Carver reached the last wagon. "Undo the canvas," he directed.

Meachum and Banner jumped to obey.

"Do not try to trick me," Slash Nose warned harshly. "My warriors will kill many whites today if you do."

Carver smiled, confident of his ace in the hole. "In a few moments you'll see that your distrust is misplaced."

Fargo knew exactly what "Mr. High-and-Mighty," as Smithers had called him, was thinking. Although Carver had gone to great lengths to avoid handing the whiskey over, he'd brought it along in case he was left with no other choice. Carver figured he would give it to Slash Nose, and that would be that.

Dulcie jumped when Fargo touched her arm. Putting a finger to his lips, he motioned for her to move toward the bank. She, in turn, tapped Paula and Tricia, but they both paid her no mind. They didn't want to miss what was happening.

Fargo's carefully laid plan was unraveling. He needed to get the women, Smithers, and Timmons to safety before all hell broke loose, but he just couldn't get their attention. And in another few moments it would be too late.

"There you go, sir," Banner said, stepping back from the wagon.

Jace Carver climbed onto the seat and shoved the canvas aside. "Here are the two cases you requested, Slash Nose," he said, bending down. "You and the other bucks can—" Carver stopped, consternation erasing his smugness. "What the hell?"

"Where is my whiskey?" Slash Nose demanded one last time.

Fargo grabbed Dulcie and pushed her. "Run!" he whispered. "Down over the bank!"

Carver was frozen in shock. He had straightened and was staring at the Pawnees as if he had no idea what to do. Finally he blurted, "Your whiskey isn't here." It was the wrong thing to say.

Slash Nose suddenly threw back his head and screeched like a hawk, and from out of the trees whizzed a flight of feathered shafts. In a twinkling, five guards were down, one man thrashing wildly with an arrow through his throat.

"No!" Jace Carver yelled. "You don't understand!"

Slash Nose wasn't listening. He had swung onto the off side of his war horse and was goading it toward cover. A guard rushed to stop him, only to receive a blast from the brave's Sharps full in the face.

The other two warriors also wheeled. One was brought down by a volley from the guard's Spencers, but the other shifted on his mount and unleashed arrow after arrow, rapidly notching and loosing the deadly missiles.

Fargo grabbed Paula and Tricia and propelled them toward the blonde. "Go with Dulcie!" he instructed them. Then he ran toward Smithers and Timmons, who were mesmerized by the escalating violence.

The guards were firing blind into the trees, blasting away at anything and everything, while arrows continued to streak from the underbrush.

Jace Carver was still atop the last wagon, sitting there dumbfounded. Below him, Meachum and Banner banged off random shots, protecting their employer as best as they were able.

Fargo's hand fell on Smither's shoulder. "Run! That way!" he hollered, pointing at the women. "It's your only hope!"

The butler did as he was told but the mousy little secretary balked, crying, "I can't leave Mr. Carver! He might need me!"

"For what?" Fargo responded. The man could be of no help whatsoever. "If you value your hide, go with the others!"

Timmons was a study in indecision. "I don't know what to do!" he said. At that moment the matter was taken from his hands by an arrow that caught him high in the ribs, piercing his torso and jutting out from the other side. One instant he was alive and well, the next he was dying on his feet. His lips moved but no sounds came out as he tottered, then sprawled onto his stomach.

Back-pedaling, Fargo whirled and sprinted toward the bank. Slash Nose had promised not to harm him, but that was no guarantee one of the other warriors might not get caught up in the heat of battle and try to slay him. He covered twelve yards when lead whistled past his head and shoulders, missing him only because he had veered to the left to avoid a cottonwood.

It was no accident. Stopping, Fargo spun and jerked up the Henry.

Jace Carver had risen and was jabbing a finger at him, screeching over and over, "Kill him! Kill Skye Fargo!"

As always, Meachum and Banner had obeyed without question. Meachum fired again, the slug nearly clipping Fargo's ear. Banner's pistol was now empty and he was furiously ejecting spent cartridges from the cylinder.

"Kill him, damn it!" Carver railed.

Fargo settled a bead on the center of Meachum's sternum and smoothly stroked the trigger, the Henry kicking only slightly as it spewed lead, smoke, and death. Meachum was jolted against the wagon, his bowler tumbling, but he tried to shoot once more. Fargo's next round lifted the easterner on his heels.

That left Banner, who finished loading and adopted a two-handed stance for greater accuracy. The Henry boomed and a hole materialized in his forehead. His legs melted beneath him as his body collapsed.

Bedlam reigned. Half the guards were down, dead, or wounded. Horses plunged and reared and whinnied in fear. Above the madness rose the rumbling roar of Jace Carver. "Someone get me out of here! That's an order!" But the guards were too busy fighting for their own lives to give any thought to his. Jace had managed to pay for both the service and obedience from his servants, but much like the sun, their loyalty would rise and set without ever becoming his. Even if they had an ounce of loyalty for Jace, it was doubtful anyone could have prevented what happened next.

Slash Nose stepped into a gap between two cottonwoods and his Sharps thundered.

Like a kite caught in a gale, Jace Carver was catapulted from the wagon seat.

Fargo resumed back-pedaling. A glance showed him that the women and Smithers had made it over the bank. But they were far from safe. Slugs and arrows flew thick and fast, and the outcome hung precariously in the balance. It was then, at the frenzied height of the battle, that the clarion notes of a bugle heralded the arrival of the patrol that had been shadowing the supply train since it left Fort Kearney.

Captain Travers was at the forefront, leading the charge that brought the conflict to a swift end. Those Pawnees still alive fled, some bolting on horseback, others bounding like antelope, with the soliders in grim pursuit. Carver's men were ordered to drop their weapons and herded together.

Fargo stopped on the lip of the bank. The three women and the butler were below, Smithers with his arms draped protectively over the ladies. All four were safe and sound.

A prancing bay, caked with dust, was brought to a halt beside Fargo. "I've got to hand it to you, friend," Captain Travers said. "Your plan worked just as you claimed it would. You should be proud of yourself."

"Should I?" Fargo said, staring at the arrow protruding from Timmons.

Dulcie Rose stood. "Is it safe to climb on up there?" she asked. "Is it over?"

"Almost," Fargo replied.

The mopping up took another half an hour. Slash Nose and his three warriors had been taken prisoner and were placed under guard. A burial detail was formed, for red men and whites alike, and when the patrol started back for Fort Kearney they left eighteen fresh mounds of earth to mark the spot where the richest, most powerful man in Kansas City had learned there were limits to what wealth and power could claim.

On their arrival at the post days later, the entire garrison turned out to meet them. Captain Travers had sent a messenger on ahead to inform Colonel Ainsley, and word had spread like wildfire. Soldiers packed the parade ground to cheer the victory of their comrades-in-arms. Even the hospital staff came out to applaud and whoop.

The excitement and confusion explained how one particular patient was able to stagger from his bed, swipe a rifle left leaning against a wall by a careless trooper, and make his way to the entrance.

Fargo had just helped Dulcie down and faced the commanding officer when a single shot pealed. The slug meant for him tore into Dulcie's mare, digging a furrow in its flank. In a blur, Fargo drew and fired.

Guzman was fumbling with the rifle, attempting to lever another round into the chamber. Smashed against the door, he oozed onto his side, astonishment the last emotion to stamp his features.

"*Now* it's over," Skye Fargo declared to no one in particular. No one said a thing, no one moved, as he grabbed hold of Dulcie's wrist and barreled toward the sutler's. He needed a good, stiff drink. Later, he would take the blonde up on her offer to spend a night together, or maybe go her one better.

A couple of days with a willing woman could make a man forget anything.

LOOKING FORWARD!

**The following is the opening
section from the next novel in the exciting
Trailsman series from Signet:**

THE TRAILSMAN # 227
NAVAJO REVENGE

*New Mexico Territory, 1860—Fort Fauntleroy,
situated between* Dinetah *(Navajoland)
and the* malpais *badlands:*

Slavery, no matter who is the slave, is evil.

The cavalry had been after Skye Fargo for three days.
The rangy, lake-blue-eyed man known as the Trailsman dismounted from his Ovaro and walked to the
edge of the steep-walled red sandstone mesa, and
looked down the slope at the blue-clad column struggling along the twisting trail. A bright New Mexico-
summer sun burned at his weathered face and caused
sweat to run in small rivers from his brow. Fargo
wiped it away with his bandanna unconsciously.

He heaved a deep sigh and knew he could not keep
running from the U.S. Army for long. They were too
determined to find him. Settling on a rock, he let his

Ovaro rest while he took in the incredible view of the
territory. Two of the Navajos' three holy mountains
lay to the west and to the north, rising majestically
amid a purplish haze. Far to the east lay Santa Fé,
but it was a fool's errand trying to pick it out because
of the winding mountains and the *malpais,* the blackened volcanic stone badlands that turned ordinary
land into deadly stretches only the best—or most desperate—could cross.

The Trailsman was the best, and even he found the
going hard.

He cocked his head to one side and listened to the
horses' steel shoes clicking against stone, the rocks
dislodging and tumbling a hundred feet down to the
desert floor, the creaking of saddle leather, and the
swearing of the troopers. Taking a deep breath, Fargo
caught the scent of sharp sage with a hint of sweat
and lather from the horses. For three days they had
pursued him. Fargo had just wanted to enjoy the sce-
nery and relax for a few days, but the army had been
persistent. It was definitely time to find what such ded-
ication meant.

The leader of the column struggled over the mesa
rim and spotted Fargo immediately. If the Trailsman
had wanted to hide, this cavalry captain would have
hunted throughout the territory for a hundred years
and never found so much as a hair from Fargo's head,
but Fargo thought it was time to end the chase, as
much for his own peace of mind as for the struggling
horse soldiers.

"Howdy, Captain. What can I do for you?" Fargo
said.

"Mr. Fargo, you're a hard man to run down. Why
were you trying to get away?" The captain dismounted, took off his canvas gloves, and tucked them
under his broad black leather belt. The man was older
than Fargo had thought from the easy way he rode,
perhaps in his early forties. He had a direct gaze and

an honest face. This bothered Fargo even more because he knew what the captain was going to ask of him.

"I don't want to scout for the army," Fargo said. "That's what you were going to ask, wasn't it?"

"You read more than trails, sir," the captain said. He thrust out his hand. Fargo shook it, noting how firm the captain's grip was. "I'm William Chapman, commanding officer of Fort Fauntleroy."

"The new fort right at the edge of Dinetah?"

"Yes, sir, that's the one. We're at the periphery of Navajoland and entrusted with keeping the peace."

"The Navajos have been peaceable enough of late," Fargo said. "They might skirmish with the Pueblos, but I haven't heard anything of them raiding settlers."

"That's been changing, and it's not just because we built the fort," Captain Chapman said. He settled down on the rock next to Fargo and enjoyed the same view for a moment. Fargo wondered what Chapman saw.

The Trailsman saw frontier, wild and free and open for a man to make a name for himself or to just pass through. Fargo worried that the captain saw something else. A land to be settled, plowed under, and armed, fenced off and grazed. A land for cities to sprout up like toadstools after a rain.

"What's changed," Chapman went on, "is the slave raiding. The Mexican settlers are complaining that their women and children are being taken by the Navajos. The white settlers call the Mexicans *los ricos,* because they've got established spreads and more money than they can shake a stick at."

"Slavery's going to eat this country up alive," Fargo said. Men—and women and children—had to be free. Not ought to be, *had* to be. That was the way he lived his life and the way he believed everyone ought to.

"The Navajos claim *los ricos* are stealing *their* children and hustling them out of the territory, taking them south into Mexico. And now the white settlers are claiming the Indians and bands of slavers are preying on *their* women and children. It has to stop."

Fargo said nothing. The captain was right. Such inhumanity had to be ended.

Captain Chapman turned and stared earnestly at Fargo. "Sir, I won't mince words. I need your help. I need the best scout I can get to track down whoever's responsible so I can stop the slave trading."

Fargo had not been sure what the captain was going to use as an excuse to recruit him as a scout. He had worked for the army before and many times it had been a tough and dangerous job. Still, people he knew and respected got along all right with the military. Kit Carson, working as an Indian agent over in Taos, had no fight with the army. If anything, he helped whenever he could. Other mountain men of Fargo's passing acquaintance had worked for the army, too. Ceran St. Vrain even boasted of it, but then he would boast about making the sun come up, if anybody would listen to his tall tales.

"Pay's terrible. Food's even worse. Fort Fauntleroy has just gone up and lacks many of the amenities of more established posts."

"So what's in it for me?"

"Satisfaction at doing your duty, Mr. Fargo. That and twenty dollars in danged near worthless scrip a month."

Fargo sighed. "With such generous terms, how can I refuse?" He thrust out his hand, and the captain shook it.

Fargo looked past the cavalry officer at the vista stretching forever. This was his kind of place, where he could stand and imagine riding anywhere in the world. A young child stolen from his mama and papa and put into slavery would never share this feeling of utter freedom. He had to see to changing that.

Fargo mounted his Ovaro and started to work right

away, leading the column down another, less steep trail, and headed directly back to Fort Fauntleroy, his new home for a while.

The town just outside Fort Fauntleroy, Ojo del Oso, was pleasant enough. The construction didn't seem much different from any of a dozen other places in New Mexico Territory: mostly adobe, with some attempts to erect stone houses and buildings. The people were friendly and greeted him as he rode through. Fargo saw a few whisper to friends and relatives as he passed. Fame was a bit hard to bear, especially when he had not done anything to deserve it among these fine people.

"You must be the new scout over at the fort," greeted a florid man with muttonchops, all the rage back East, or so Fargo had been told.

"I am."

"Come on into my store," the man said, ushering Fargo inside the adobe building. "Even if you don't buy anything today, it's cooler inside than out. That sun can dry a man's brain."

Fargo stepped into the dim cool of the general store and looked around. He needed some ammunition for his Henry rifle, and maybe a blanket to replace the one he had used for more than a year. It had become threadbare and the merchant had some fine Two Grey Hills Navajo blankets.

"You like 'em?" the man asked. "I traded for those blankets off a soldier who captured them during a raid."

Fargo ran his hand over the fine, distinctly patterned wool blankets, then moved on. If a soldier had "captured" them, he might also have stolen them. Fargo wanted no part of that, since it might incite any Navajo he came across. Captain Chapman had told him his job as post scout was to find slavers, track them to their lair and then bring down the full might of the U.S. Cavalry on their heads.

"Reckon all I need today is a box of ammo for my rifle," he said.

"Here, it's on me. I'm Austin Kincaide, fort sutler. I'll put it on the captain's bill." The man smiled broadly, showing a gold tooth in front.

"Papa, aren't you going to introduce me?" came a voice like wind blowing through the tall ponderosa pines. Fargo turned to face the woman in the doorway leading to a back room. He touched the brim of his hat.

"Ma'am," he said, eyeing her. She was a real armful, this filly. Several inches shorter than Fargo, she had eyes as blue as the sky and lustrous blond hair that fell below her shoulders. Her oval face seemed too fair for anyone living in Ojo del Oso, but Fargo was not complaining. This young woman was a vision of loveliness.

"That there's my younger daughter, Dorothea."

"You have another daughter? If she is half as lovely, you are a man doubly blessed, Mr. Kincaide."

"Aren't you the charmer?" Dorothea said, moving forward, her skirts softly sweeping the floor of the store. She smiled prettily, then eyed him the way he had been eyeing her. Dorothea seemed to like what she saw as much as Fargo did.

"Luella's betrothed," Austin Kincaide said, "but Dorothea is an old maid. The ugly duckling of the family."

"Old maid?" Fargo's eyebrows arched at this. "Ugly duckling?"

"Why, I'm only twenty-two, Papa. That's not so old. Do you think I'm too old to marry, Mr. Fargo?"

"Never too late," Fargo said.

"Luella's got herself pledged to Jack Sawyer. Perhaps you know him," Kincaide said. "He works at the Silver Centavo."

"He's a cardsharp and a cheat," Dorothea said acidly. "Don't make Texas Jack out to be anything more, Papa."

"You're just jealous of your sister. Now git on into the back and straighten up, child, like I told you."

"Very well, Papa." Dorothea batted her long eyelashes at Fargo before turning and going. As she vanished into the back room, she looked over her shoulder. The smile she gave him was anything but demure and set Fargo's pulse to pounding.

"Don't pay her no nevermind. She and Luella never got on too good, even being sisters and all. When their ma died, it sort of drove them apart."

"Don't think you have anything to worry over, Mr. Kincaide. Your daughter's likely to find herself a beau. A woman that pretty won't go unmarried for long."

"She's had offers from the officers at the fort," Kincaide said, almost too hurriedly, as if explaining Dorothea's unmarried condition like he might some disease. "But she didn't take to them, though I think she looks favorably enough on the captain."

Fargo heard someone enter the store and wondered at the flash of anger that passed over Kincaide's face. The store owner hurried to the man, a Zuñi from the look of his clothing, and the two spoke in low tones for several seconds. The more Kincaide talked, the madder he got.

"Anything else I can do for you, Mr. Fargo?" he called.

Fargo picked up the box of cartridges for his rifle and tipped his hat in the sutler's direction. Almost immediately Austin Kincaide went back to his whispered argument with the Pueblo Indian. Fargo stepped outside into the hot sun, again aware of how fast a man might die in this country. His tongue felt like it had been wrapped in cotton and he needed a beer to wet his whistle.

Fargo headed for the Silver Centavo Saloon down

the street. He was more interested in seeing who Dorothea's sister was marrying than getting a beer, but he had gone only half the distance when Captain Chapman came galloping up, his horse lathered and the officer agitated.

"Mr. Fargo, glad I found you. There's been another raid. Out near the Zuñi pueblo. A half-dozen young boys were stolen away by Broken Finger at a nearby watering hole."

"Who's Broken Finger?"

"A Navajo trying to make a name for himself as a war chief. Manuelito and the other chiefs won't have anything to do with him. He's just trying to prove himself."

"The Zuñi village about fifteen miles from here?" asked Fargo, walking to his horse and swinging into the saddle. He settled down, reached back, and dropped his shells into the saddlebags. It was a good thing he had not had that beer. It might have robbed him of needed senses.

"That way," Chapman said, pointing to the southwest. "We'll be riding fast, so I only brought a dozen men with me."

"I can make better time on my own," Fargo pointed out.

"Mr. Fargo, it would be best if the cavalry handled the matter of the slavers."

Fargo shrugged. He understood what the captain said—and didn't say. The brass over at Fort Union wanted the cavalry to settle the matter to enhance their prestige and power in the area. Fargo found it more tedious riding with the soldiers and worried that the raiding party might slip back into the rugged Canyon de Chelly. Not anyone, other than a Navajo venturing into that red-rock spired canyon, ever returned.

No one.

"Let's see that watering hole," Fargo said.

* * *

"What do you make of the tracks?" Chapman asked Fargo.

Skye Fargo stood and walked along the dusty trail. Rock and sand made tracking almost impossible, but now and then a horse stepped into the dirt or made an impression that remained, even after a puff of wind came to erase it.

"Indians," Fargo said. "They are riding in that direction." He pointed due west.

"I'd think Broken Finger would hightail it for the safety of Canyon de Chelly."

"You just might have it backwards, Captain," Fargo said. He took off his floppy big-brimmed hat and waved it through the air so the sweat would evaporate and cool him a mite. For three miles Fargo had followed this trail and could only come to one conclusion.

"What are you saying?" demanded Captain Chapman.

"Looks as if the raiders are Zuñis, not Navajos."

"But you said there were Navajo tracks!"

"There are. If that's Broken Finger, he's chasing after the Zuñis, not running from them," Fargo said. "That's where the Zuñis took four or five young children from a Navajo band of mostly women back at the watering hole, where we found evidence of the fight."

"That's not possible. Everyone knows Broken Finger is the one taking the slaves."

"Not saying he doesn't have a few," Fargo allowed. "What successful Navajo warrior doesn't have a couple wives and a few slaves? But the slavers this time are the Zuñis."

"Might you be wrong about this?"

"Might be," Fargo said, "but I don't think so." He put on his hat, pulled down the brim to shield his eyes, and looked into the setting sun. A particularly rocky area drew his attention. This was the sort of place where water pooled, bubbling up from underground hot springs. And the kind of place Indians out on the trail stopped to rest.

"Are the slavers ahead?" asked Captain Chapman.

"Let me do some scouting," Fargo said. "If I signal, you come running. Fast."

"All right," Chapman said, not liking the way Fargo liked to do things on his own, but seeing no way to get around it.

Fargo set off at a gait his Ovaro could maintain all day and long into the night, but mostly he wanted time to study the trail and think. Everything seemed turned upside down from what the captain had told him. Fargo slowed and studied trampled grama grass and the dirt under it for a spell.

For the world, it looked as if the Navajos pursued the Zuñis. The Navajos weren't called the Lords of New Mexico for nothing, having superior horses. At times, Fargo marveled at their horsemanship. The Zuñis were less well versed, being farmers tending crops instead of warriors ranging far and wide across the countryside. The horses in the lead group of eight seemed weaker, smaller, less able.

Before he reached the tumble of rocks where he thought the Zuñis might have camped, he dropped to the ground and left his faithful Ovaro tethered to a low-growing mesquite. The pinto contentedly nibbled at the bean pods still hanging on the limbs, deftly avoiding the long spines.

Henry in hand, Fargo hurried forward, reaching the rocks. He had almost an hour before sunset. The Zuñis might have watered their horses and then ridden on, but Fargo did not think so. He was not sure they even knew the Navajos were on their trail. The Zuñis might have decided to camp by the watering hole.

If so, this place could have turned into a bloodbath.

Like a snake slithering through the rocks, Fargo moved forward until he spotted scrubby cottonwoods growing beside the pool of water. A crude rope corral held eight horses, confirming the number Fargo had thought. And to one of the trees he saw three small Navajo boys with ropes around their necks and their hands bound behind their backs.

They sat stoically, eyes ahead and showing no emotion. He knew what they must feel inside. Not one was older than seven or eight years old. Fargo started circling the camp where the Zuñis laughed and joked, sharing a rabbit. Bones from two others had been tossed to one side.

The Zuñis feasted but offered nothing to their captives.

Fargo's finger tightened on the Henry's trigger, but he could not take out all the Indians before they began fighting back. He needed the extra firepower offered by the cavalry if they were to rescue the boys and ensure their safety. Especially if the Navajos hadn't arrived yet.

He climbed to the top of a boulder some distance from the Zuñi camp and lifted his rifle, waving it over his head. Dust kicked up in the distance, telling him Captain Chapman was on the way. Fargo returned to the Zuñi camp, just to safeguard the young boys.

Just after he wedged himself into position into the rocks, where he could look down over the camp and take a decent shot at any Zuñi trying to harm the boys, all hell broke loose.

From three sides came whooping, hollering braves. Fargo blinked in surprise when he saw that only three Navajos attacked the eight Zuñis. He lifted his Henry and sighted in on one Zuñi, shooting him before he could drive his knife into the back of a Navajo warrior.

The Navajo twisted around, saw the dead Zuñi fall, then looked into the rocks and spotted Fargo. Their eyes locked, onyx and lake blue, and there was no camaraderie. Though outnumbered, the Navajos fought fiercely against the Zuñis until Chapman and his squad came storming up.

The bullets flew and ricocheted, and took out two more of the Zuñis. The Navajos did not retreat, even when the cavalry charged up. As they fought on, it was the Zuñis who fled.

Chapman ordered some of his men after them, not seeing that the three Navajos, bloodied from the uneven fight, were now sidling around the watering hole toward the captive boys. From his perch, Fargo watched the Navajos use their sharp knives to slice through the ropes.

The boys were free. Again the leader's eyes locked with Fargo's. Fargo touched the trigger of his Henry, then lifted the barrel and just waited.

No thanks, no sign of gratitude. The Navajo leader—who must have been Broken Finger—slipped into the gathering shadows with his two warriors and the rescued slaves.

Skye Fargo wondered what he had gotten himself in the middle of.